MW01135220

This book is a work of fiction. The names, characters, places, and incidents are products of the writer's imagination or have been used fictitiously and are not to be construed as real. Any resemblance to persons, living or dead, actual events, locale or organizations is entirely coincidental.

When trouble walks in, there's no choice but to hold on tight for the ride.

Two years before, Shaw Woodward watched the love of his life walk down the aisle to another man. Since then, life has kicked him in the balls and lifted him up several times. Just so happens he's on the downward dip of that cycle right now.

After a difficult mission in the Ranger Ops unit, he's struggled to keep his focus, and his captain is forcing him to seek help. He just never expected to walk into the shrink's office to find the woman he loved seated behind the desk in sexy secretary glasses with her blonde hair in a confining bun he wants to unravel.

Atalee Franklin has experienced a lot of highs and lows lately — a marriage and a divorce to name a couple. As a psychologist, she's passionate about helping people through their most difficult moments, but then in walks Shaw, the gorgeous, muscled friend of her ex-husband, and also some of the reason her marriage failed.

With another shot at a relationship in his sights, can Shaw actually get his head clear enough to move forward? Leaving the Ranger Ops isn't even a possibility — the only way they'll strip him from the unit is by putting him in the ground. Atalee only wants Shaw to find peace while doing something he loves, though her worries for him are real. Losing him a second time isn't even an option...

WITHIN RANGE

by

Em Petrova

Prologue

Two years ago

"Are you gonna stand here and let this happen?"

Shaw's father gave him the sideways look that meant he'd better fix his disposition and do it fucking fast.

He tugged at the collar of his dress shirt. It felt uncomfortably tighter with each second that counted down to the wedding ceremony.

"What are you talking about?" Shaw shot back. But he knew—and playing stupid wasn't going to fix the situation. The woman he loved was walking down that aisle, and it wasn't to him.

His father squared up with him. Lawdy, this situation was going downhill like a pig in a mudslide. His father looked him in the eyes, and his voice came out low and intense.

"You love that woman. Have for years. Why the hell are you letting this happen? You don't get many chances at happiness in this life, son."

1

Shaw stared over his father's shoulder toward the altar, where his buddy Johnny stood alongside his brother as best man, suited up and waiting for the first strains of the wedding march.

Without looking at his father, Shaw muttered, "I can't just stop the wedding."

"So you're going to stop your life instead?"

The words struck Shaw like a hail of bullets, each finding its mark deep within him.

Goddammit.

He turned from his father.

His black leather dress shoes tapped out a beat on the floor that mirrored his heart. Stained glass flashed by his vision and he stepped through a doorway into the bridal suite.

A gasp sounded as Atalee's female entourage saw him standing in the doorway, but he couldn't see a fucking thing but the bride in white, her honey blonde hair piled in an extravagant updo with little fucking flowers tucked into the strands and a floor-length veil.

Dammit.

"I need to speak to Atalee alone," he grated out.

Her eyes found his, big and sea green, the depths filled with surprise.

He was about to surprise her even more, and with any luck, three hundred wedding guests when she cancelled her wedding and ran away with Shaw.

2

The bride's mother touched her arm, and she gave her a nod and smile. The women scuttled past Shaw, and he threw a glance over his shoulder to ensure they wouldn't overhear what he was about to say.

As he moved toward the most gorgeous woman he'd ever seen in his life, his throat dried out. He swallowed hard and stepped up before her.

"Atalee…"

With her face tilted up to his and wearing all white, his heart threatened to give out from pounding so hard.

Kiss your bride.

She's somebody else's bride.

Dammit to hell.

"What is it, Shaw? Is something wrong?" Her soft-spoken manner took hold of him by the balls. This woman owned him, pure and simple.

He grabbed her hands, hovering over her with the urge to kiss her so fucking strong, he didn't know if he could even speak. Emotion threatened to close off his throat, but he wasn't a quitter or a coward. He was a fucking Texas Ranger, and he wanted this woman with every cell of his being.

"Atalee, you can't marry Johnny."

She blinked up at him and paled slightly. "What happened? Did he back out?"

"No, no, nothing like that," he rushed to say before she lost more color from her face. His heart flexed hard, painfully. "Atalee, I've known you for years now."

Confusion creased her blonde brows. "Yes."

He was fucking this all up. *Just say it*, he ordered himself.

"I can't let you walk down that aisle and marry Johnny. Because I'm in love with you."

A beat of silence followed, and her sea-green eyes widened.

"Baby doll, I can give you everything you ever wanted. I'm better for you than the man out there." He gestured toward the main part of the church where all her guests were expecting her.

She dropped her head and stared at the bouquet she held. The petals of the brightly-colored flowers trembled in her shaking hands.

"Shaw, why are you saying these things to me? Why did you wait so long? We've known each other for years."

"Because I can't let you marry another man without telling you how I feel. I can't watch you destroy your life with someone who won't love you the way I do."

She took a step away and then another. His instinct was to grab her back, yank her flush to his body and kiss her with all the passion flowing inside him. Three long years he'd wanted her. Johnny had been his friend for much longer. They'd trained together as Texas State Troopers, but only Shaw had

4

gone on to be a Texas Ranger. All the while, Shaw had known Atalee as a driven woman as well as a sweet one, while she worked diligently to finish her Master's of Psychology so she could move on to get her doctorate..

His chest inflated as he gathered wind to speak, to somehow convince her to walk away with *him*.

"Atalee, listen—"

Her face twisted in a grimace of pain. "No, you listen, Shaw Woodward. You can't just walk in here and tell me you love me minutes before I'm about to marry your friend. Hear those words? *Your friend.* What kind of man betrays a buddy like this?"

"There are sides to Johnny he doesn't show you. At least I don't think he does." Dammit, he was grinding up his words into pig slop. "Atalee, I don't think he can give you what I can. All I want is you."

She took another step away from him.

He was losing her.

Lifting the bouquet like a ward against evil spirits, she glared at him. "Get out of here and don't come back, Shaw. I'm marrying Johnny. I *love* Johnny."

Jesus Christ, those words hurt.

Shaw wasn't known for giving up easy, though. In two steps he was with her, a hand planted on her lower back as he jerked her against him and slammed his mouth over all that lipstick that another man was meant to kiss off her sweet, honeyed lips. For a moment, she stood still in his hold.

Then she melted.

Just a bit.

It was enough for him to sweep his tongue through her mouth, gathering all the flavors he knew were it for him for the rest of his life.

Till death did they part.

Suddenly, she shoved her hands against him. Flower petals crushed against his suit jacket and tumbled to the floor as she stumbled back.

"Damn you, Shaw! Leave!"

He felt his jaw muscles bunch up and knew he was getting pissed. He leveled his gaze at her. "You sure you want that? Because you felt yourself melt into my kiss just as much as I did."

"Fuck you!" She came at him, bouquet flopping on smashed stems. She hit him square in the chest, but he didn't even rock on his feet. She was an itty-bitty thing and he was six-two. Yet... who knew seeing hatred on a woman's face could bring a man to his knees?

She was fucking killing him.

"Get out of here! I never want to see you again."

He firmed his jaw and just stared at her for a heavy heartbeat. Her chest rose and fell with fury, but all he saw was the woman he wanted through thick and thin. It might be their first fight and later they'd laugh about it.

6

"I don't have feelings for you, Shaw, and I never will. Now go." Her eyes narrowed to slits, and her words were venom darts, striking him one by lethal one.

He brought a fist to his lips, pressing back any words that he might say to ruin her life even more than he already had. In the end, he gave a nod, sent her one last look that would have to suffice for the rest of his days and walked out.

On the way to the front doors, he walked past his father, who caught him by the arm.

The wedding march was playing, and he turned away from the sight of Atalee drifting up the aisle on her own father's arm to meet her undeserving groom.

"Did you talk to her?" his father asked quietly.

He nodded. "Didn't do any good."

Tossing one last look up the long aisle, he found Atalee looking back at him before she turned to Johnny and joined hands with him.

Shaw walked out. Then he went straight to the Texas Rangers' office and put in for a transfer, which he got three weeks later.

Chapter One

"Jesus. Not another active shooter situation." Shaw ducked his head back around the corner. "I got no visuals, Sully," he said into his comms device.

This particular armed gunman had holed himself up in the thick of the downtown district. Between SWAT teams, fire departments and the damn media that seemed more eager to get their story than to take their next breath, the vicinity was crawling with people.

"We'll get you into a better position. Woody, Linc, get closer and keep low. Jess, Cav, head east and get eyes on the windows," Nash Sullivan, captain of the Ranger Ops special forces unit, ordered in response.

"Where the hell are you, asshole?" Shaw scoured the front of the building. Shots had been fired from the fifth or sixth story and crumpled out two pedestrians approaching the building entrance.

With Linc at his side, Shaw ran in a crouched position through a courtyard area. Linc pulled up beside him, head tipped back to the windows across the street.

"C'mon, you fucker. Show yourself," Shaw muttered. One flash of a scope in one of those windows, and Shaw would end this here and now. He kept his sights trained on the front of the building, but it was possible a lot worse shit was about to go down inside.

"I think we should go in," Linc seemed to echo his thoughts.

"I'm with Linc," Lennon said.

"Damn, I know you're my twin but do you gotta copy everything, bro?" Linc said to his brother through the comms.

"Yep, that's how I nailed your girlfriend last night," Lennon shot back, a grin in his voice.

"Keep the chatter down," Nash responded. "But yeah, we need to get in there. Lennon and I are breachers."

Shaw peered through his scope, moving from window to window yet saw not so much as a shadow. Most of the windows reflected the street back to him, but he was trained to see things most people couldn't. Hell, after only nine months in the Rangers Ops, he could even see ghosts.

"We're in." Nash's voice came at them, low. Seconds later, tension filled his tone. "We need Cav."

Shaw and his partner on his three, Linc, shared a look. This couldn't be fucking good. If the captain needed Cavanagh, he'd run across something that most likely had a fuse and a detonator.

A short popping noise stiffened Shaw's spine, coming from deep within the walls of that building. "What the fuck is that, Sully?" he demanded.

"Shooter's on the move. Get in here. Now!"

The four of them converged and hit a back entrance. In a blink, Shaw assessed their surroundings and gave orders to search the floors, starting on the fifth, where the shots were suspected to have come from while Cav took off to locate the explosive.

A trickle of sweat coursed down Shaw's neck, swallowed by the collar of his tactical jacket. It was hot as Texas in the dead of August in here, and it didn't have anything to do with the layers he wore, along with his bulletproof vest.

"Cav, it's mighty hot in this place. You thinkin' what I'm thinkin'?"

"Yeah, I fucking am."

The explosive could be tripped by temperature fluctuations.

"There's more than one guy at work here. Watch your sixes," Nash ordered.

Shaw, Linc and Jess took the stairs two and three at a time until they reached a steel door at the top. Jess raised his brows at Shaw, and he gave the nod to go.

They'd just breached the door and were fanning out, heads moving right and left, when Cav let out a whistle.

"Not any garden variety fertilizer here, guys. This is enough fucking explosive to bring down aircraft."

"Missiles?" Shaw asked at once under his breath.

"Damn close. Housing's different, to make it more vulnerable."

"That's where the heat comes in. Shit, can somebody get to the boiler room and get that A/C back on before we all end up stains on the earth? Jess?" Nash's order had Jess splitting off from Shaw and Linc.

They moved in precise steps along the stairwell. A squelched scream had the hairs on the back of Shaw's neck on the rise. Slowly, Shaw pushed open the door and he and Linc rushed the corridor. Office doors leading from it were mostly shut, and the open ones were empty.

"What the hell is this building? Who works in it? Someone important? Or is someone important visiting today?" Lennon asked. "This is enough explosive to make a big statement. This is not just a pissed off employee but the work of a group."

"A very organized group too," Cav drawled out as he worked over the bomb.

"So why the shooter? Why not just cut the air and walk away, letting the place rocket off the map?" Shaw firmed his jaw as the words left his lips. His pulse was tripping again, and he had to concentrate on keeping his head on straight. He couldn't fuck up at a time like this, lose it like some weenie rookie who wet his pants at the first sign of conflict.

He bit the inside of his cheek, and the sharp pain helped him focus a bit. Weapons raised, they swept a room.

"Marco," Linc murmured.

Of course nobody answered Polo.

"I'm not playing any fucking games," Shaw barked out, sweating heavier now. The base of his spine was soaked. Damn, he had to stay on task. This wasn't at all the same as Mexico. He wasn't going to gun down another teenager.

That shit had haunted the hell out of him, and he'd been battling for months now. Despite the fact the kid had a bead on Shaw and was about to shoot him between the eyes didn't make it any better to his mind. He still couldn't shake the memory of turning the guy over with his boot and finding him a lot fucking younger than he'd thought.

"There." Linc's breathed out word was barely audible even a step away from Shaw.

"Get the son of a bitch down, but make sure he's not wired first. Cav, Lennon and I would like to keep our balls." Nash's words barely registered in Shaw's ear as he stepped out around the corner and got a good look at the shooter.

Shaw closed one eye and took the shot.

The gunman hit the ground in a slump of dead weight, and a woman screamed. She jumped up and ran at Shaw. Weapon aimed, he prepared himself to squeeze off another shot before realizing it was just a woman dressed in office attire.

No. It was that teen boy from Mexico. Shaw stared at her, watching her face shift to the youthful angles and —

"Goddammit," he swore at himself. Sticking out one arm, he grabbed the woman and swept her up against the wall, shoving her down. "Get down, under that desk and stay there, you hear me? There might be more shooters."

"Shhhiiiit, this is one hell of a computer system on this explosive," Cav was saying during all of this. "Jess, you got that air back on yet? We need you up here."

"Shaw hit a mark. I'm approaching the body now," Linc said.

Shaw watched his teammate move toward the crumpled form before realizing he should be watching for other threats.

Dammit, he was going to have to break down and get that help Nash kept haranguing him about ever since Mexico.

Linc nudged Shaw again. "Good shot. Clean."

His mouth filled with bile, and for a second, he battled the urge to go make sure it wasn't another kid he'd shot, even though he knew otherwise.

Yes, definitely needed that shrink, even if he and every man he'd ever worked with balked at sitting on a couch and having their childhoods probed when all they really needed to do was stop questioning whether they should have killed somebody who'd asked for it.

"Jesus Christ." Jess's oath filled Shaw's ear. "Who the fuck's in the place? The amount of explosive here, someone wants him not only dead but his DNA wiped off the planet."

"Cav, Jess, Lennon, take care of it. I'm going to meet up with Woody and Linc to find out," Nash said.

Ten tense minutes later, they'd flushed out one more shooter. Nash hovered over the disarmed man, his boot pinning him firmly to the patterned carpet of what appeared to be a law firm.

Each question he fired at the man had him turning more purple with rage, but he refused to loosen his lips and talk.

"He's no good to us. Finish him off," Shaw drawled, turning away from the scene.

His bluff had the guy squeaking out, "Wait!"

It took a bit more coercing from Nash in the form of a stomp to the balls and a broken nose, but the information they received was exactly what they were looking for.

Shaw stared at Nash as he spoke to the others. "Seems like we're about to be heroes, boys. We just pegged the goddamn nationalists who've been moving arms around to hate groups." That kid in Mexico had been part of it too.

Shaw kept his weapon trained on the captive, who glared up at him defiantly. "Want me to watch this asshole while you go with Linc and find out who the target is?" he asked his captain.

Nash gave him a hard look, and it wasn't until Shaw saw his captain's eyes flicker with warning that Shaw realized he was in a rage.

"First lieutenant." Nash's use of Shaw's title snapped his head up. "I got this guy covered. You go scope out the building."

The rest of the mission blurred together as they searched the building and got the word from Cav that the explosive had been neutralized. The bomb squad was on their way in to remove it, and Shaw and Linc got all the workers inside the building rounded up and put into a few large rooms to be questioned.

Nash pulled his comms device out of his ear and gripped Shaw's shoulder. "Look..."

Knowing exactly what he was about to say, Shaw cut him off. "I'll go this time. I got it."

Eyeing him, Nash gave a hard nod. Then he stuffed his communication device back into his ear.

Shaw couldn't shake the image of that woman's face shifting into the teen's. Why the hell weren't the other guys fighting some demon? They'd all made kill shots too.

15

Shaking his head, he moved out. His part of the job was done for one day and he could get on with his life.

Pressing his lips together, he followed the others out of the building, past the media and police barricade and to their SUV.

Fuck—had he really just told his captain that he'd find a head shrinker? If he didn't, he'd risk losing it on the job worse than he already was.

* * * * *

"Dr. Franklin."

Atalee looked up at the sound of her name to see her receptionist standing there holding a bundle of paperwork. She suppressed a groan, because her desk was already littered with things she'd barely glanced at but needed attention. So far, she was loving her new position with the VA hospital, but she was failing at staying organized.

She smiled at the receptionist, who'd been very welcoming with her so far. "Thank you. I'll take them." She got up and circled her desk to accept the stack of what was files and mail.

"These are your new cases for the week."

"Thank you."

The receptionist glanced at her desk. "Would you like me to file anything for you?"

Atalee gave her a smile of appreciation. "Not yet. I'll let you know when I've tackled more of it."

She breezed toward the door. "I'm only here until three today."

"Thanks for letting me know."

Atalee dropped the entire stack to her desk with the rest and let out a sigh. Since she was pretty well caught up on all the new patients she'd seen this week and she didn't have another for an hour, she could take the opportunity to clean up her desk.

Setting her hands on her hips, she looked around. Where to begin?

Her first week on the staff of the social services department had been a whirlwind. Thrown directly into the job by landing in the ER with a patient within the first hour had not only wet her feet but dunked her completely. She'd been officially baptized, and all her caring instincts had instantly risen to the surface.

She looked forward to helping as many vets as possible. And with all the depression, traumas and mental health issues those who had fought for their country dealt with, she was in the perfect position to help.

With an idea in mind of where to begin tackling her clutter, she dragged an extra chair toward the side of her desk and began sorting things into stacks — files, mail and items she wasn't sure what to do with yet.

Halfway through, she unearthed her doctoral certificate matted in the expensive frame her mother had gifted her after she'd been given the honor.

Touched once more, she looked around and discovered a nail in the wall behind her desk, left over from the former clinician who'd held this position.

After hanging her degree, she returned to her task. The first piece of mail she picked up had her stopping dead, her heart hammering in her chest.

Swallowing hard, she skimmed over the law firm on the return address. Her mouth dried out as she realized what she was holding.

Her final divorce decree.

Atalee set it aside for a moment. Then picked it up again. Guilt flooded in at the very sight of it—a failed marriage, that if she was honest with herself, she'd played an active role in ending.

She wouldn't get anywhere by ignoring things. *Don't stuff it down*, she often told past patients from the family practice she'd worked at for years while finishing her doctorate.

Biting the bullet, she tore open the envelope and withdrew the sheet of paper. A flick of a finger had her reading the words.

Quickly, she folded the paper and placed it back into the envelope. Yep, divorce decree. It was done—finally. After almost a year of waiting, painstakingly splitting her life apart from Johnny's, she had freedom.

Too bad it didn't relieve the guilt she bore. Since day one of their marriage, she'd had questions and a lot of what-ifs. What if she should have postponed the wedding? If she'd waited just another day, week, month, would things have worked out?

What if Shaw Woodward hadn't barged in before her nuptials and said those things to her?

It was Shaw who had pushed over that domino that had begun the effect of unraveling her ties to Johnny. No, he hadn't just tapped the domino—he'd shoved it with enough might to rock her world.

Many times she'd relieved those moments—so often she wasn't certain anymore what she'd embellished in her mind or what was real.

She set the envelope on the desk in the only clean corner and stared at it a moment. *I'm sorry, Johnny.*

She was. But he'd done his fair share to ruin their relationship too. The times he shut her out completely, using passive aggressive actions to hold her at arms' length. Still, she always wondered if that might have begun with her. After all, she'd kissed another man on her wedding day. And she'd listened to what Shaw had said about Johnny not being able to love her the way Shaw could.

Even now his deep voice reverberated inside her mind, raising goosebumps on her arms. She could still feel the stroke of his gaze and the hard way he'd held her against him right before he'd kissed her.

Whoooeee, had that man kissed her.

All virile strength, power and intensity rolled into a muscled Texas Ranger.

Before that moment, she'd never thought of Shaw as anything but Johnny's friend who came around often enough that she considered him her friend too, and they invited him to barbecues and to root for their favorite baseball team.

But the minute he'd stumbled over that speech to her, telling her that she was marrying the wrong man and Shaw couldn't let her walk down the aisle without knowing his feelings... her universe had flipped on its side. She'd felt like a beetle pushed over, unable to find the ground beneath him and with legs churning helplessly.

The first weeks of her marriage, she'd probably spent too much time remembering how Shaw's steely lips had felt across hers. Her energies should have gone into Johnny.

Sometimes, she stopped blaming herself enough to realize Johnny wasn't the same man she'd met back while obtaining her master's degree. He'd swept her off her feet, been attentive and they'd had a lot of fun together.

But had she actually married *that* man? Or had she just grown comfortable with him and spending five grand on a wedding dress seemingly the next step in life?

She didn't realize she'd sorted through the entire pile of paperwork until her fingers brushed the wood top of her desk.

How was it that even two years later, Shaw could affect her so much? Her nipples were bunched up

20

inside the silk cups of her bra and that low flutter was back in her belly.

She looked to the envelope, sitting all by itself on the desk. She was free.

Free to find Shaw if she wanted to.

It's been two years. He'll be married or in a relationship.

Suddenly tired by the thought, she sank to her desk chair and assessed not only the state of her desk but her life. Too bad having a doctorate in clinical psychology didn't mean she had her own shit together. She supposed it was all a journey, though. As she assisted patients in resolving issues, she had a new venture to embark on as well, a chapter without a husband.

She needed to move forward without Shaw jumbling her thoughts too.

From now on, whenever she thought of the man, she'd control her physical response to the memory of that kiss. From now on, Shaw Woodward didn't have a hold on her.

Chapter Two

Shaw tipped back his beer and watched as two of his teammates stepped up to the head of the lanes. He lowered his beer with a chuckle. "What the hell kind of form is that, Linc? You getting ready to walk the catwalk?"

"Shut up, Woody. I saw it on ESPN."

Shaw, the rest of the guys and Nash's fiancée Nevaeh broke out in laughter. Linc took a rapid approach and released the ball.

"Holy shit." Nash stood and watched the ball rolling straight for the head pin. The crash of it striking—and wiping out—every pin had Linc turning to them with a smug expression and a middle finger in the air.

Shaw rubbed at the back of his stiff neck. "I take it back, man. Your new form is obviously working for you."

Linc's former bowling scores from their weekly gathering here at the Pins 'n Sins hadn't been on the losing end of the spectrum, but the man was competitive enough to watch the most boring sport on ESPN to gather tips and tricks.

"I'm grabbin' another beer. Anybody need one?" Nash looked to his pretty little woman, who was on her feet and rotating her ball to find the holes for her turn.

"I'm good." She gave him the gentle smile of a woman in love.

"I'll stay and watch you roll first, darlin'." Nash raked his gaze over her figure in a way that had Shaw looking away. That it had been a hell of a long time since he'd bedded a woman cut a path of acute awareness through him.

When Nevaeh stepped into position to throw, Nash moved up behind her and clutched her by the waist, pulling her back against him as he lowered his mouth to her ear.

"Get a fucking room, guys," Linc said with a rumble of a laugh.

"At least someone's gettin' some action," Shaw drawled out.

Linc and Lennon gave him twin stares, their expression the identical one of shock. "You gotta get out more, bro," Linc commented.

"Look." Lennon pulled out his phone and drew up an app. With the swipe of a finger, five pretty girls were on the screen. Lennon passed a thumb over one image and then sat back against the hard plastic booth seating. "Easy as that."

"Dude, that's like shopping for a steak."

"Easier." Linc swigged his beer.

Nash threw them a glance and stepped away from his woman. She rolled a seven and got a round of applause for her improvement, as bowling wasn't her forte. Nash brushed a kiss over her forehead and moved off to the Sin part of the Pins 'n Sins to get his beer.

Nevaeh came back to the seat, and Shaw gave her a high-five. She grinned and sank down with her beer.

"You've been practicing?" he asked.

"Nash and I have come here a few times, yeah." She gave him a sidelong look. "Where have you been hiding yourself, Shaw?"

He suppressed a grunt.

Not her too. Nash was riding him enough about his current preference for going home alone. There was nothing written in stone saying a single man had to attend every party this side of the Mississippi and bang a new woman each night. What was wrong with hitting his recliner with the Rangers ball game on TV?

Nevaeh let it drop, thankfully, but it only made him think on how supportive she was to him and the rest of the Rangers Ops team. If she doled out kind words and pep talks to them, Nash must have the Holy Grail of support from her.

Shaw's mind shot to Atalee.

Fuck, he hadn't given her more than a passing moment of thought in so long, but her image leaped into his mind as if he'd just seen her the previous day.

24

How those lush lips, honey-blonde hair and sea-green eyes never faded from his memory always shocked him.

On the heels of the shock—and a primal stirring of desire in his gut—was a healthy dose of regret.

He never should have said those things, and on her wedding day.

After all this time, he could still see that searing look of anger in her eyes. He didn't know if she'd ever told Johnny about it or not, but Shaw hadn't stuck around long enough to find out. He'd never spoken to his friend again and transferred to another part of Texas with the Rangers. If that was being a coward, then he'd take the title without complaint.

The few times Shaw had allowed himself to think on Atalee, he'd wondered if she'd finished the degree that was so important to her and whether or not she and Johnny had popped out a kid by now.

That thought always got tucked away to a dark corner of his mind, where no sun could shine. Fact was, he could never be like Linc, swiping an app to hit up a girl later. Not when he was still as in love with Atalee as much as he'd been two years before.

"What are you doing later, Shaw?" Nevaeh's words cut into his brooding moment.

He lifted his beer as a reflex, hiding his discomposure. After a sip, he lowered the bottle and shrugged. "Dunno. Maybe go for a run."

"Your ass better hit that track, dude. You're fallin' behind me in sprinting drills." Lennon's remark brought a twinge of a smile to Shaw's lips. The last two drills Nash had put them through, Shaw and Lennon had been neck and neck.

"You only won last time because your gigantic big toe went over the line first."

Lennon didn't seem to care. "A toe's a toe."

"Shaw, you're up." Cavanagh came back from rolling a spare.

"Hold my beer." He passed it to Nevaeh with a grin and grabbed his ball. These times with the Ranger Ops team gave him a sense of family, and whether or not they knew it, he felt calmer afterward. The ghosts of what he'd done in Mexico to that teen didn't seem to touch his life while in the Pins 'n Sins. Maybe it was the good company or the constant crash of balls that did the trick, but he was glad for the reprieve.

Soon enough he'd be back home with the constant weight of the situation bearing down on him. Only today might be different—after the incident in the office building, he'd seen no recourse but to find that therapist and get help. As captain, Nash couldn't allow it to continue and would need to recommend he be let go from the team, and Shaw couldn't imagine returning to the life of a Texas Ranger again. No, it was guts and glory for him now—his life as a Texas Ranger was over. Checking immigration papers and serving warrants seemed too tame for the man he'd become.

A strange thought. Had he changed that much? He had.

He drew back his arm and released the ball, sending it whizzing down the slick floor toward the pins, barely registering the cheer that went up behind him as he knocked down all ten, leaving a gaping hole like a carnival clown game with missing teeth.

He put some extra swagger into his walk as he returned to the seat. Nevaeh high-fived him.

"You should let me make you an account on this app," Linc said. "Bio—sharpshooter who's good with his balls."

That had them all roaring with laughter, and even Shaw couldn't contain himself. The lighter moment chased thoughts of Mexico, and Atalee away too, thank God.

Nash returned with another round of beer for all of them. "This is just a warm-up for the whiskey I'll be serving at my place." He turned to Shaw. "Steaks and whiskey after this, man."

"Thanks, but I gotta pass."

Nash had become one of his closest buddies since they'd been sent to the Sabine River to neutralize a threat. That encounter had formed bonds between them that later had gotten them onto the brand-new special forces team formed by Operation Freedom Flag Southern US division, or OFFSUS.

Shaw gripped Nash's shoulder. "I got someplace to be."

"I hope it's getting laid. Time to live up to your nickname of Woody," Linc quipped from behind. He took another beer from the six-pack Nash held and sauntered over to the ball return.

"Wouldn't you like to know more about that?" Shaw drawled with a flash of a grin.

Linc gave him the finger.

Nash looked to Shaw. "I hope it's a good someplace."

"Actually, I'm late and I don't have time to finish my game. Nevaeh?" He looked around Nash to the pretty woman watching Linc's catwalk pose again.

She looked up with a smile.

"Take over for me, doll."

"I'll ruin your handicap."

"I'll live with the flak I get from these jerks." He moved to kiss her cheek goodbye and gripped hands with Jess, Cavanagh and Lennon in farewell. "I'll see you pussies on the flip side."

Then without hanging around longer, Shaw left.

The drive to the VA hospital was one he'd driven a few times with his father when the Vietnam vet had issues with his knees. But he'd never been there for his own reasons, since he wasn't military.

Or technically, he now was. Still, he'd used his newfound ties to set himself up with an appointment with a therapist who was supposed to be top-notch in dealing with vets with stresses and other mental issues. While Shaw was not that bad off, at least to his thinking, he *was* eager to unload this burden of guilt and get on with living his life.

* * * * *

Shaw's initial impression of the Office of Mental Health's waiting room was a general feeling of gloom and despair. A few guys slumped in chairs, staring at their hands or into space. One who was leafing rapidly through the pages of a science magazine was bouncing his knees nonstop.

Looking around for the check-in desk, Shaw felt the beige walls close in on him. His heart kicked up its pace, and now he knew why that guy was jiggling so much—the place made Shaw's skin crawl too.

As he approached the window, the girl looked up with a smile. Then she blinked quickly. "Um, can I help you?"

"Shaw Woodward for Dr. Franklin."

The list of doctors to choose from had been short, and he'd chosen Franklin right off the top, because Atalee's last name had been Franklin... before she'd married Johnny. Shaw must be a motherfucking masochist.

"Ah yes, our newest clinician on staff. Just fill out these papers please." As the receptionist slid the clipboard through the window to him, she did another eye-batting thing. Maybe she had something caught in her lashes or the Texas cedar everyone was known for being allergic to was getting to her.

Shaw accepted the clipboard and snagged a pen from the cupholder. He took a seat as far from the others as possible, which left the four of them spattered through the room, each as anti-social as the next. Maybe it was a necessary trait to get through the shit they had to experience. Don't get too attached, because your buddy could fall at any time.

Or you could wipe out an entire group of kidnappers, human traffickers and online thieves along with a criminal teenager and end up fucked in the head for months afterward.

Shaw's general mood made him press hard on the page, and the pen nib dug in, tearing a hole in the paper. He pushed out a sigh and continued filling in the address, medical history and so on.

When he returned the clipboard to the lady at the window again, she blinked several times at him. He looked closer—her eyes weren't bloodshot.

"Dr. Franklin will be with you soon."

He nodded and moved back to his seat. The science magazines someone believed would attract vets' attention did nothing for him, so he just sat there staring at the patterns in the beige carpet, darker tracks that wove through it like an ant farm he'd had as a kid.

While he sat there, he tried to keep his mind from wandering toward reasons he should get up and leave. He clearly needed this — he had no choice but to speak to someone. With luck, it would be a one-off and he wouldn't have to return.

Briefly, he thought on Nevaeh finishing out his game and wondered what score he'd ended up with, and that led him to thinking about the guys at Nash's place, having whiskey and ribeye steaks.

He felt his own knee bouncing and shot a look at the other guy, who was now drumming his fingers on his thighs that jiggled up and down.

Suddenly, the receptionist appeared in front of him. He took in the lines of her body. A printed dress skimmed slight curves and ended at sculpted calves.

"Dr. Franklin will see you now. Come with me." Her voice had a higher pitch.

He stood and she began blinking again. Damn, it seemed the entire place had some tic or another. He followed her through a door and down a hallway. She paused at a door to rap softly. A voice on the other side answered, though Shaw couldn't make it out, and she popped her head in. "Your patient, Dr. Franklin."

"Thank you."

It wasn't a man's voice.

When the receptionist stepped aside, Shaw moved to the open door. His heart gave a wild lurch, like a chained animal leaping at a trainer behind a fence.

The woman seated behind her desk had the same thick blonde hair as Atalee. She wore a light blue cardigan primly buttoned up to the neck, and glasses gave her a sexy secretary appeal that any man's dick would react to.

Then Dr. Franklin looked up and locked eyes on him.

Fuck.

Fuck.

Fuck, it's her.

*   *   *   *   *

Atalee couldn't find a single breath of air in the entire room. Her lungs burned and spots started to waver before her eyes, flashing over what was the most rugged and sexy man she'd ever laid eyes on.

Except she *had* laid eyes on him. She'd even kissed him on her wedding day once upon a time.

The need to draw air hit her, and she sucked in a breath. Gripping the edge of her desk, she got to her feet. Her receptionist still stood there, and Atalee waved toward her. "Thanks, Danielle."

The man stared at her. She stared back. Danielle closed the door, leaving them alone. The last time they'd stood like this, he'd told her he was in love with her and she shouldn't get married.

32

Turned out, he was right.

"Atalee." The way he grated out her name, like he was dragging rocks over concrete, had all the hairs on her arms standing on end.

"You're not Joe Beck."

"No." Hoarse. So perfectly rough, like his hand on her back had been against the silk of her wedding gown. "I gave a false name – at least on that form."

God, she had to get a grip on her emotions. She felt like a glass that had fallen off a table and splintered into a thousand pieces. Dragging those shards close and putting herself back together was essential right now, for her, for Shaw, who'd come here for help under an alias.

What was he even doing in a military hospital?

"How… how did you get past the military part to even get here?" She stiffened her fingers to keep them from visibly shaking, but nothing would help the shivers taking over her stomach.

"I am military."

Her gaze rode over his cowboy hat, a ridge top style he always preferred, then across his features, each as hardened and chiseled as the next. When she reached his lips, she quickly scuttled past it to his angled jaw stubbled with five o'clock shadow. He wore a blue denim shirt open at the collar, cowboy-style, and jeans settled perfectly low over his hips held in place by a belt with a buckle bearing his name.

A gift from his daddy. All the Woodward males had a buckle like that, a rite of passage or something, she remembered him telling Johnny what seemed like a million years ago.

A long heartbeat passed between them. What had he last said? Oh yes, he was military.

All she could think about was how much she wanted to hug him.

Snap out of it and be professional.

"When did you become military?"

"When did you finally become a doctor?" he returned, bright blue eyes washing over her like a caress.

She swallowed. "Sit down, please."

He did so, hesitantly, hovering over the sofa cushion for a second. God, he was bigger, more muscled, rougher around the edges—and fully capable of turning on all the dials of her libido that had been non-existent ever since her marriage had turned sour.

Shaw stared at her without pause, and she moved from her desk to the comfy chair she used to speak to patients on a more personal level. Two friends talking about life. Except in this case, she didn't know if it was possible to speak to him—or even treat him, for that matter. It was a conflict of interest when she'd thought about Shaw's mouth moving over hers, down her throat to suck at her breasts and finally lower, between her—

She gave the entire heap of her thoughts and emotions a firm shove away.

The crease of Shaw's jaw worked, an instant reminder to that moment in the church. "How's Johnny?" he grated out.

Damn, could her heart beat any harder? She was going to need a lie-down on her own therapy couch after this, just to recover from the exertion this man had put her through.

"I don't know," she said quietly. "I'm divorced."

Was it providence that she'd gotten her decree just the other day and now Shaw was back in her life? She'd always been a believer that people invited things into their lives when they were ready. What did that say about her case?

"Divorced." He leveled a look at her.

She nodded. Crossing her legs, she smoothed her trousers over her thighs and hoped Shaw couldn't read the confusion she was feeling on her face. For years, she'd worked to keep her reactions off her face, because she couldn't show shock or disappointment in what a patient was telling her.

Somehow, she felt Shaw was seeing right through all that.

Time to take control here.

"Tell me what you've been doing. You left the Texas Rangers?"

"Not exactly." His hand, in a relaxed fist, settled on his thigh.

His very thick thigh, straining against his Levi's.

She swallowed.

While to outward appearances, he was calm, she noted how his lips tightened at the corners.

"Okay. Well, what brings you in here today?" Even if she couldn't help him due to their personal connection, she had him here and he clearly had come for a reason. The idea that he needed real help from her made her heart flex.

He was silent a moment, his eyes roving over her face.

A flush stole over her, and she hoped to hell it didn't land in her cheeks and reveal what she was feeling.

"You were referred here because I listen to men and women who've seen combat and struggle to process some of the things they've seen or done. Is this the case with you, Shaw?"

He was quiet, his brows not quite drawn together but pretty close.

"If you don't feel you can confide in me because of our link, then I totally understand and can provide you with a referral to one of my colleagues. Dr. Eris is very well known for—"

"No. You're good."

Why did that word—good—seem to fill some void inside her? The tension in her belly tightened like a vise.

Atalee wet her lips, and his stare locked onto her mouth. The flipping sensation low in her body had her mind skidding off the tracks again.

"Look, Shaw. I really shouldn't speak to you since we are — were — friends."

"I'm with a special ops unit," he said at once.

His admission pinned her back to her seat. "That's different."

"Yes."

"I'm assuming that's why you're here."

He hitched a boot over his knee and shifted on the sofa. It was impossible for her to stop looking at him like a woman looks at a man she's attracted to. No, not just attracted to — gut-wrenchingly crazy for. Scratching an itch with this hard, broad Texas Ranger turned special ops man was everything she'd been dreaming of since she and Johnny had split.

"My father sold off all his horses," Shaw said.

She rolled with the abrupt change in topic and nodded. "Was it something he'd been planning for a while?"

"Not really. But ranchin' is hard, especially small operations like our family's, and I guess he realized it was best to get out while the numbers in his checkbook were still in the black."

She contemplated him and the subject matter. He clearly wasn't ready to discuss his true reason for coming to therapy, and she was okay with that. She'd seen it before, many times in the family practice she'd worked at. Sometimes it was a deflection, an ice breaker. Other times it was the patient's way of avoiding the touchy subjects and stalling. Either way, she was listening.

That smooth drawl of Shaw's had her body coming to life. How many times had she turned those words he'd said on her wedding day over and over in her mind? Countless.

As he continued to speak, telling her about how his father had lost one of his favorite horses to old age, and then up and sold all but a few, Atalee focused on the man sitting before her, the man she'd never expected to see again—the man who'd suddenly popped back into her life.

Chapter Three

What the ever-lovin' hell was Atalee doing here? And divorced. Jesus.

Had Johnny hurt her, the way Shaw had always believed he would? Shaw was ready to storm out of the building, find the man and personally mop the floor with him for all the things he imagined he'd done to hurt this woman.

She was free.

Dammit.

As he talked, he couldn't tear his gaze from her. How was it that two years had only amplified her beauty? She'd grown into her loveliness with a grace and self-confidence she hadn't had before. The way she sat with her legs crossed so elegantly and those glasses perched on her face had Shaw's cock shoving at his fly.

"Does it make you upset that your father sold the stock? Was it your dream to someday inherit and run the ranch?" She removed her glasses, holding them by the stem in one hand as she looked at him head-on.

He might as well be looking down the barrel of a 50-caliber — the effect she had on him was just as devastating.

"Would be some years before I could take over the ranch. I never had plans for that — I always wanted to go into law enforcement."

She nodded. Her hair was pulled back at her nape with some loose tendrils framing her face. What he wouldn't do to tug that band loose and let all her hair down into his hands as he slanted his mouth over hers.

"You could still buy more horses and start it up again, in time." Her comment was lost on him a moment as he got over-involved watching her lips, imagining all the ways he could kiss her. Soft, nibbling... or with long swipes of his tongue.

He gave a nod. "Guess I could. My dad kept a couple, though, for ridin'. Said he couldn't go cold turkey from rancher to empty barn."

Why was he talking nonsense?

Because he couldn't bring himself to say what he really wanted — which was that he still fucking loved her.

He sat forward, elbows on his knees. "Look, I'm not here because I'm crazy."

She set her glasses aside on a small table and looked at him. "Coming to see someone for help doesn't make you crazy, Shaw."

Damn, did she have to speak his name that way — all breathy and warm, so he thought of laying her back on a mattress and gliding into her tight heat?

"Those guys out there — I'm not like them."

"No two people are alike."

His chest felt weightier than when he'd entered the room. He couldn't talk to Atalee — she was too close to his heart, and he couldn't risk letting her see more things to dislike about him, when she probably already hated him for what he'd done on her wedding day.

Shoving to his feet, he looked down at her. "I'll move on."

"Wait. Shaw, if you can't speak to me, then at least let me refer you to — "

"There are other coping mechanisms to explore, and I'll find them."

She moved to stand as well, following him to the door. He wrapped his fingers around the handle, battling the surge of need to turn and pull her into his arms. Her light perfume wafted to him.

"Shaw, there's no reason to go this alone, and clearly you or even your superior officer has reason to bring you here. What happens here in this room is about you finding peace with whatever brought you here in the first place."

He couldn't look at her for fear of lifting her, spinning her to the door and pinning her against it.

But he felt her nearness like a flame licking over his skin.

If he didn't leave now, he never would.

He twisted the handle and opened the door.

"Thanks for your time, Atalee."

"Shaw."

He paused with a boot over the threshold.

"Next week, same time."

Fucking hell.

He nodded and walked out. He must be a goddamn lunatic to agree to see her again, but even as he thought it, he was acutely aware of the very excited pounding of his heart.

* * * * *

Atalee closed the door and leaned on it. Bringing one hand to her lips, she fought to control the dark need Shaw had raised in her with his gritty tone. Seeing him again, and so soon after her divorce was final, had her mind skipping like pebbles across the surface of a pond. The ripples on the surface of her being were only what was visible—deep down, she felt the bigger waves and all she could do was hold onto the side of the life raft.

What had brought him here? Her eyes were trained to see things patients attempted to mask from the world. The tightening of his fist on his knee, the tension in his shoulders and that solemn mouth of his showed her more than he probably cared for her to see.

She wanted to help him, because Shaw was a good man and deserved all the happiness he could find for himself, even if that had nothing to do with her. She could remain professional enough to treat him — she knew it.

Though, a slippery stirring between her thighs made her question her own motives. If she was honest with herself, she felt too hot all over, as if he'd just cornered her in that bridal suite again and kissed the daylights out of her.

She sent a look to the sofa where he'd been sitting, imagining how ruggedly striking he looked. Changed, hardened.

You were right about Johnny, she wanted to call him back to tell him. *He couldn't love me the way I needed it.*

All of a month had passed following her honeymoon for her to realize the man had quickly sunk into old married ways, plopping on the couch with the remote and unable to give her the attention she needed in order to feel loved. Shaw had known that long before they'd tied the knot, it seemed, but how?

She gathered herself enough to walk out to the receptionist desk.

Danielle looked up with a smile. "Oh my goodness, Dr. Franklin. That man... he gave me shivers!" she whispered.

"Uh. Yes. He's quite good-looking." *Understatement of the decade.* "Did he happen to schedule another appointment?" She leaned over to point at the calendar.

"Yes, he did, along with a note."

"What's the note?"

"Could cancel."

Atalee gripped the edge of the desk. Could cancel because he might change his mind about returning? Or something could pull him away from his personal life, make him abandon everything but duty?

She had his file, but he'd admitted to giving false information on the form he'd filled out at the front desk. Though, the hospital was very strict about its patients, and no way would he have gotten away with falsifying documents for them, which meant he was in the system.

A thought came to her. As his therapist, she had the right to pull his files and dig into his background. Special ops unit—who was he with? The idea of him as a bad-ass hero sent her body into overdrive all over again.

No, she couldn't pry into his life. Either he would come back and talk to her or he wouldn't. Either way, she had to come to terms in her own mind with both eventualities.

Throughout the rest of the afternoon, she was focused on her next patients, though the seconds between offered her too much time to think on Shaw.

She could still see his broad spine as he stood at the door with his back to her. How she'd wanted to rest her hand between the planes of muscle and let him know he'd been right about Johnny and things had gone downhill quickly.

But she wasn't so sure if she wouldn't still be married to him if not for Shaw's interference that day. She'd let the man get under her skin, made her second guess her choices and maybe that had caused her to see things in Johnny sooner, to place higher expectations on their relationship, which only set him up to fail.

The guilt was still a heavy stone roped around her neck and when she walked out of the hospital for the night and got in her car, all she could think of was taking a run. She needed the exertion, the pounding of her feet on pavement to carry her mind away from all this.

Once inside her small house nestled in her quiet neighborhood, she shed her sweater and trousers in favor of spandex and a slim-fitting tank top. The evenings were still just as hot as ever in Texas, and most people didn't like to run in the heat, but going to the track at the gym today wasn't for her. She needed to be alone.

She soaked a bandanna in icy water and wrung it out before knotting it around her neck. Then with her water bottle strapped to her waist, she locked up her house and took off.

Every step matched her heartbeat, and that was still entirely too fast. After seeing Shaw, it hadn't slowed. The skin on her arms pebbled despite the temps. She lengthened her strides and turned the corner, stretching her legs on the next block.

How did a Texas Ranger get reassigned to a special ops unit? There was a story there, one she was dying to hear. She couldn't pry a single word from that man, she knew. Next time, he'd probably talk more about ranching and horses, about his father, who he'd always been close with since his ma passed several years before Atalee had ever met Shaw.

Her trained mind lingered over aftereffects of his mother's death and how they played into the person he was now. But Shaw was also a driven man. He'd probably walked out of the womb ready to take matters into his own hands, and no wonder he'd landed himself in a position where his duty was to take action.

Atalee turned another corner, whizzing past houses with minivans parked in the driveways and moms yelling at kids to hurry up and buckle their seatbelts so they could get to soccer practice. Normal American lives of normal American families. And here she was—feeling like a screwed-up mess despite her abilities to help patients cope with their own problems.

She'd gone over it all so many times—Shaw had interrupted her wedding, planted a seed of doubt. That had sprouted roots that had grown quickly into more doubt and within six months, the fighting with Johnny had been intolerable.

Shaking her head, she tried to cast off the entire mess. It was quicksand she'd never dig her way out of once she started analyzing her mistakes. Sometimes it was best to move on, to forgive and forget — or to pay her own therapist a visit.

The heat was getting to her, and the wet cloth around her neck was now like hot water. She didn't slow, though, because it would just prolong her time out here. Instead, she found that inner strength to keep going, her pace set to help her reach home and find a cold shower as fast as possible.

When she rounded the corner, her house came into view. The last few steps in the heat sapped the final drops of her energy, and she slowed.

Then she saw him. A man sitting on her front step, knees splayed and his elbows resting on them. Her heart gave a little jog of its own before recognition smacked her.

Shaw.

God, she looked like a sweaty beast that had just finished a rainforest marathon and the man she'd dreamed about nonstop was waiting for her on her front steps.

How had he found out where she lived?

Atalee couldn't even fix her ponytail in a way that didn't seem as if she was primping. At her approach,

Shaw looked up. Pain creased his brows, and she stopped in her tracks.

Finding her voice seemed an insurmountable task. She wet her dry lips and managed, "What are you doing here?"

He stared at her a minute, eyes combing over her body and leaving behind a quake like a lover's touch. Then he unfolded his long legs and got to his feet, tugging his cowboy hat brim as he did. She wished he wouldn't do that—hide his eyes from her.

"What are you doing runnin' in this heat? You're going to collapse. Get inside in the cool air." His command shouldn't send shiver after shiver racing over her skin. Or maybe that was heat exhaustion. Either way, she did need to cool off.

She stepped up to the porch and fished a key from a little zipper on the waist of her spandex running pants. He watched her insert it and open the door. She glanced back to see if he was following, and he was.

God, the tension inside her made her feel she was about to crack.

"That's the only lock? You don't have more protection than that?" He pointed to the door.

She shook her head. "This is a good neighborhood and—"

"You treat patients who could be mentally unstable, Atalee. They could follow you home."

She stared at him. "Shaw, you're my patient and you followed me home."

Agitated, he waved a hand. "I didn't follow you."

"Which means you have ways to find out where people live," she stated.

He looked at her without giving anything away.

"Come in. I need a drink and a shower before we talk."

He closed the door behind him and twisted the lock. The action—the veins bulging down his forearm—had her thinking indecent thoughts. Fact was, he now was her patient and he shouldn't even be here, friend or not.

She was not going to even allow her thoughts to touch on what else Shaw could be to her... what he once had wanted to be.

When she walked to the kitchen and poured herself a glass of water from the filtered pitcher, she offered him one as well, but he shook his head. She raised the glass to her lips, and he watched her drink.

Lowering the empty glass, she looked at him. "Why are you here, Shaw? Wait—don't answer that. I really could use a shower." Sweat was rolling down her back and even her thighs. "Here, take a glass of water and hang out a while. Okay?" She poured him a glass and forced it into his hands. When his callused fingers grazed over hers, her body temp raised another few degrees.

He just stood there, watching her.

She must look really terrible. She pointed to the kitchen chair. "Have a seat here or in the living room."

Without waiting for his reply, she hurried to her bedroom and grabbed loose black shorts and a gray T-shirt with her school's alma mater logo. In her bathroom, she turned on the cold water and let it run a moment while she stripped. She wasn't even going to glance at her reflection. She already knew she must be beet red from the heat and her own discomposure at finding Shaw at her house.

He was in her kitchen, drinking from her glass.

She was twenty steps away, totally naked.

Her nipples pebbled, and she stepped under the spray. The splash of cold water hit her skin and cut through the sweat, but it did nothing for the internal warmth spread low through her belly, the awareness that in the other room was a gorgeous man who could rock her world.

After a cursory wash, she stepped out and toweled herself. There was no help for the wet hair — she'd have to wait for it to air dry, which was her secret pleasure anyway. Any time she could skip over the trappings of modern women — like makeup, bras or hairdryers — she did.

It was actually something Johnny had hated, often asking her if she was going to sit around the house like that, and part of her did it now as a way of casting him off. Clearly, she still held on to some animosity when it came to that man.

As she dressed, she considered how Shaw had known the real Johnny and she hadn't. Or if she'd just turned a blind eye to it all so she could tick off the next thing on the to-do list of life and get married.

Stopping those memories was easy when she turned to open the door. Feeling cool and as light as air now, she went back to the kitchen. Shaw hadn't moved and the water was untouched.

At her entrance, he locked his gaze on her. He blinked, a slow closing then opening of his eyes. She stood there a moment, bare feet glued to the ceramic tile. Then she peeled them off and walked to the fridge again. This time she took out the sweet tea and poured a glass. She raised the pitcher in offer, but he shook his head.

Leaning against the counter, she sipped. "Look, Shaw, you're here for something. If it's to talk about the things we didn't cover today, that's okay. We have plenty of time. I mean, I should really refer you to another doctor. It's a conflict of interest to treat you since we know each other, but—"

"Atalee." He grated out her name in the roughest of ways.

She set aside her tea.

"I couldn't part ways without telling you I'm sorry," he said.

Part ways? Where was he going?

"Sorry about what?" she asked the obvious question.

51

His direct stare started to pick apart the threads holding her together. One by one, she felt them pop until she had to drift to a chair and sit down.

"You know what, Atalee. Your wedding day. I never should have said those things to you. It was wrong of me, and I've regretted it ever since."

Those weren't exactly the regrets she'd experienced over the years. Shaw had been that man who'd spoken up even without the minster asking if any man objected to her and Johnny's union. Shaw's intervention had opened her eyes and might have saved her many more years of suffering in a marriage that wasn't healthy.

"Shaw, you don't have to apologize—"

"I do." He took her hand.

God, it was huge, swallowing hers. She stared at the backs of his knuckles, lightly dusted with dark hair. And the veins that snaked over his hands and up his forearms to disappear into the rolled sleeves of his western shirt had her hyperaware that anything she said could be used against her in a court of law... but might get her laid.

"I shouldn't have ambushed you that way."

"Well, I'll admit it wasn't perfect timing."

"It was for shit." The corner of his lips twitched as if he might smile and seeing a smile on this man's face again would splinter her heart into a thousand shards of joy.

"There's no need to apologize, Shaw. It's over, water under the bridge." She was aware her words were clichés that she'd been trained not to use on patients. Right now, though, Shaw was her friend.

She drew a ragged breath. "You said something about parting ways."

He slanted a look away. "Never know what I'll run into. I can't leave things unfinished."

"So you came here to tell me this in case something happens to you." Her words came out flat, along with a sharp pang to her heart.

He shifted his stare to their joined hands, and then he brushed his thumb over hers, barely a rough tingle over her skin.

Oh Shaw.

Whatever happened now, he was right—things couldn't go unspoken. Too much time had been lost between them already.

Her muscles tightened, and she had to shove down the urge to jump into his lap and hold on tight for whatever ride was to come.

* * * * *

While Atalee had been in the shower, Shaw had found himself battling to stay away from that bathroom door. He'd prowled her house, checking the security of windows and door locks, and luckily it had helped him control himself.

But now… sitting across from her with her soft hand in his, it stripped another bolt out of the hardened machine he tried to be in her presence. Just looking at her, all girl-next-door in her college shirt and no fucking bra… Jesus, how was he supposed to remain cool at all? Hell, he had a raging boner beneath this little antique farmhouse table, and the woman had no goddamn clue what she would be into with him in her life.

Her wet hair was beginning to dry on her shoulders, the ends growing wispy and curling. So freakin' soft. She wasn't wearing her glasses, he'd noted upon first seeing her run up to the house, and she wasn't wearing them now.

"Where are your glasses?" he asked to cut off the need inside him. It didn't work. Nothing fucking would.

She angled her head at his question. "I put in contacts for running."

"That brings me back to the question of why the hell you're running outside in Texas. Do you have a death wish? Do you know how many Rangers I've seen collapse and you're half their weight."

"I doubt I'm half." A smile brushed across her full pink lips. "I usually use the track at the gym, but I couldn't face all the people today."

Ticking his gaze over her womanly appearance made him realize what a mistake it was to come here. If he didn't leave now, he'd have her in his arms and his tongue in her mouth.

He released her hand and stood.

She stared up at him, lip caught between her teeth. He stifled a groan.

"Where are you going? Sit down. We're talking."

The command in her voice almost made him smile. Damn little girl could hold some sway with those hard vets she dealt with. Not him, but many.

He cocked a brow. "As a patient?"

"As a friend." She pointed to the chair he'd vacated.

A heartbeat passed before he sank to the seat again. "Look." He took her hand too, unable to stop himself from touching her in some small way. "I was sorry about the wedding. It was uncalled for. I should have kept silent."

She looked down, chewing her lip again. "It upset me for a long time after."

"How long?"

"Till I filed for divorce. Then I sort of realized the things you'd said had been your way of letting me know I was making a bad decision. You were right, Shaw. Johnny might have once loved me, but by the time we got married, things were already skating downhill. It started with him ignoring me, then eventually he said things that hurt me, and soon I was just living with all this resentment..." She trailed off. "I'm sorry. I shouldn't dump all that on your lap. It wasn't your fault."

He clutched her fingers tighter. "I'm sorry for it all. I hate that you were hurt."

She stared up at him with those big sea-green eyes tilted ever so slightly up at the corners to give her an ever-happy appearance he wanted to stare at for the rest of his days.

Shit.

This was no good.

He got up and headed to the front door.

"Shaw!"

He reached the door before he turned to her. She stood before him, all feminine sex appeal. So beautiful. And he wanted her. Always had.

"I'll see you next week, Atalee." He pointed to one of the windows along the front wall. "Might want to have that lock checked. It's temperamental and someone could force it."

Without another glance, he walked out before he started something he couldn't stop.

Chapter Four

"Good Lord, Momma, what is all this junk?" Atalee scoped out the wreck that was her mother's bonus room. The bonus clearly was that it came with so much stuff that you couldn't walk through it.

Her mother poked her head from the closet and eyed her daughter through the light blonde strands of hair that were slowly becoming all white. "I didn't know you were coming over today."

Neither did Atalee. But after the disaster that was Shaw's visit, she couldn't just sit at home and think on it. She'd go crazy. So she'd come over to her mother's house to see if she wanted to make popcorn and watch a movie like old times, but her mother was in the thick of some cleanout process.

"What's wrong?" Her mother's sharp eyes saw everything and always had. Since the day Atalee had come home from kindergarten with skinned knees after some mean kid had pushed her off the swing, her mother had seen it written all over Atalee's face, even when she tried to hide the blood on her knees under the hem of her dress.

Reaching out, Atalee picked up a plastic basket full of art supplies. "Just thought we could watch a movie. But maybe I could help you with this project if you'd like."

Her mother gave a hesitant nod, obviously unconvinced her daughter wasn't concealing her real reason for coming. Atalee offered a smile. In time, she'd spill it all to her mother, but that would entail starting at the beginning—back at her wedding.

"Let's grab some water bottles and see how much of it we can get through." Her mother started weaving her way through boxes of shoes, handbags, books, gadgets and makeup still in packages.

"Mom, when did you become a hoarder? Why didn't I know about this room?"

"Because you never come in here. It's my dirty little secret." Her mom let out a sigh. "It's gotten a bit out of hand over the past few years, I'll admit."

Understatement of the year. Everyone had a closet jam-packed full of junk they didn't know how to process, but this was a whole lot more. Bookcases lined one wall but were piled with so much stuff, that you couldn't make out the wood anymore. And it seemed to have become a walk-in closet as well, with clothes half off hangers or lying on top of boxes.

"Wow." Atalee shook her head. If ever there was a distraction for her right now, it was this.

Her mother touched her arm as she passed on the way to get water. "We'll drink and talk and sort things into boxes."

"It's going to take a couple weeks."

58

Her mother chuckled and left Atalee alone to look around. Was this what happened to your parents when left to their own devices? She fumbled through some packaged makeup, wondering what her mother was doing with so much of it, then dropped it back into the box as her mother entered the space again.

"Where do we start?" Atalee sipped her water. After stupidly running in the heat of the day, she still felt half dehydrated.

"I guess..." Her mother glanced from box to shelf to closet with clothes dragging on the floor. "Um. This is why I haven't done anything about this room. I don't know where to start."

"I think if we get the clothes sorted and off the boxes, we'll be able to see things better."

Her momma nodded and set aside her water. They got to work, with Atalee holding up a garment and her mom shaking her head yes or no. The yes pile went back onto hangers and the no was packed away in bags to go to charity.

"Maybe I'll just put those in the garage in case there's something I might want later," her mother said.

"Oh no. That's how you got into this situation in the first place. I'll take the bags with me when I leave and drop them off myself." An hour had passed, and the room still appeared to be untouched.

"Should we get some takeout?" Momma asked.

She still felt knotted up after seeing Shaw, and food hadn't entered her mind, though it was well after dinnertime. "That sounds good. Chinese? I'll order."

"You know what I like."

Atalee took out her phone and placed the order to the local delivery joint a few blocks away. When she finished, she found her mother staring at her. *Oh no. Here it comes.*

"Was it Johnny?"

The question jolted Atalee. Her ex couldn't be further from her mind. "No. I haven't heard from him in months. I got the divorce decree in the mail the other day."

"Oh. How are you feeling about that?" Her mother's eyes, sea-green like her own, gave off an empathy that had Atalee tasting the salt of tears. She pushed them back and grabbed an empty box just to busy her hands.

"I'm fine with it. It was over long before that paper was printed."

"I know my girl and something's troubling you."

She bit into her lip and picked up an old Easter basket overflowing with makeup, new and used both. When she popped the cap of a lipstick, she found it worn down to the metal nub. "Mom! There's nothing left of this! Why on earth didn't you throw it away?"

"I might want to buy that color again, and I'd never be able to find it. This way I can just look on the bottom of the tube."

Atalee shook her head in amazement. "You realize they're going to carry you off to the nuthouse for this, right?"

They shared a laugh. The next few minutes were spent opening lipstick tubes and tossing them out or saving them in the empty box for later consideration. By then the food had arrived. They went onto the patio out back to share their meal. The sun was sinking lower in the sky, and it was cool on the shaded patio.

"So if it isn't Johnny, what is it? The new job?" her mother probed her as she picked up a dumpling with her chopsticks.

She lifted a shoulder and let it fall, mouth full of broccoli. "The job is good. I'm still getting a read on how things work, but I like what I do and the people I work with are fabulous."

"Important." Her mother had retired from her long-time position as a pharmacist, with enough money banked to travel the world for the rest of her life. Atalee hoped someday she could be as smart as her mother had been and see the world. But alone? The idea didn't appeal—she would prefer to visit places with someone she enjoyed being with.

Someone she loved.

Shaw.

The name rose in her mind like the moon would soon, hanging over her and chasing away some shadows but bringing others to her existence. Shaw was a confusing entity, no doubt about it.

"So who is he?"

Her mother's question startled her so much she nearly choked. Was she that transparent? Atalee gave her mom a nervous smile. While they'd always been close, she also didn't like to air her problems, and right now, Shaw wasn't fitting into the happily ever after category—he never had.

"I suppose I'd better spill it." She set aside her chopsticks. "Do you remember a friend of Johnny's named Shaw?"

"Yes. Handsome guy. Came to your engagement party." She narrowed her eyes. "Wait. He also barged into the bridal suite that day at the wedding. What was that about? You never did say."

After a deep breath, she lifted her gaze to her mother's. "Something happened on the day of my wedding."

"What happened?"

"Shaw told me he was in love with me."

Her mother's eyes bugged at the revelation. Even saying it aloud shocked Atalee all over again, and suddenly she was back in that moment, standing in her white dress about to marry another man while listening to Shaw spout his feelings.

"Are you serious?"

She nodded.

"Wow." Her momma sat back and stared at her. "That must have really hit home."

She nodded. "Since that day, I can't get him out of my head. It's totally wrong of me, because I was married to Johnny, but when things started to go south with him, I couldn't help but hear the echoes of what Shaw said."

"Honey, life isn't perfect, and relationships don't last sometimes. As long as you didn't act on anything with Shaw—"

"I didn't," she said at once.

Her momma nodded.

Looking to her twisting hands, Atalee said, "I just always wondered… what if, you know?"

"That's natural. And he *is* hot."

"Mom!"

Her mother let out a small giggle. "I'm older but I'm not blind—yet."

They shared a chuckle and took up their chopsticks again. Somehow, just talking about it had Atalee feeling better already, even though things were still messy with that gorgeous special ops man who haunted her, now more than ever.

"So you ran into him again?"

"Yes. He apologized for what he said that day."

Her mother eyed her. "Does that mean his feelings have changed?"

63

"I have no idea. It's complicated, and I don't know what to think. Actually, I do. Let's finish our meal and then do more organization to take my mind off it."

A smile spread over her mother's face, sending happy lines upward from the corner of each eye. "I'm glad you talked to me, honey. You know I'm always here for you."

"Don't go thinking that I won't force you to do something about that room, Mom."

She laughed. "Oh, all right! It's high time I do something about that space. I've been feeling bad about it for a while."

"No wonder." She shook her head again, thinking of the hours it would take to sort through it all. Maybe it was time for Atalee to clean out her own internal closets, to purge any guilt she had remaining when it came to Shaw. If he asked for more from her, she wanted to be prepared to jump at a chance with him, sans emotional baggage.

"Thanks, Mom."

"For what?" she asked around a dumpling.

"Helping you with your mess has shown me that I need to clean up my act too."

"You have a room in your place that looks like that?" Her mother pointed to the wall with a chopstick.

Laughing, she said, "No. But I'm ready to have a fresh start."

* * * * *

Two weeks. Shaw hadn't returned for therapy for the past two weeks, and to say Atalee was worried was like stating the summers in Texas are hot. She stared out her office window overlooking a parking lot. All the cars were lined in rows, an orderly fashion that wasn't reflected inside this hospital, let alone in Atalee's office.

What had happened to him? Was he only avoiding her... or something worse?

She slammed the door on those thoughts and turned from the window, arms folded. The days since she'd seen him had been very busy workwise—she'd finally gotten into a good routine at the hospital, and her patients were beginning to open up to her. She and her mother had also gotten through the majority of their sorting project. The next step was to have a big shopping trip to purchase baskets and things to help them organize.

The moments her mind wandered to Shaw were frequent, though. She needed to find him if only to see for herself that he was all right. If he didn't want to be her patient, she understood, but he owed her peace of mind.

Dammit, he did.

Now she was getting huffy over the situation. She glanced at her messy desk. She could stay late and clean up or leave the entire mess for Monday.

She grabbed her handbag and slung it over her shoulder, heading straight for the door. On second thought...

She swung back to her desk. Beneath a stack of files was one in particular that she hadn't dared to open yet. Shaw's—not Joe Beck. Days ago, she'd requisitioned a copy of this file. Since then, she'd vacillated between guilt for prying into his life and the urge to see what had happened to the man to bring him here.

Much would be classified, not even in a file. But there might be something else...

When she got to her car, she set the file on the passenger's seat with shaking hands. Then she called her mom.

She picked up on the third ring, sounding breathless.

"Were you working on moving those boxes of books, Mom?" Atalee asked at once.

Her mother chuckled. "No, I was outside working in the flower garden. Are you coming over to help with the room again tonight?"

"Actually, that's why I'm calling. I thought I might take the night off."

"Oh good. I could use a break. I didn't realize I raised a slave driver."

Atalee laughed. "You have to admit, the room is so much better and it will be worth it in the end."

"Yes, but we could both use a break. I hope you're going out to do young single person things. If you find a hot man, don't worry—I won't expect a phone call till Monday evening."

"Mom!"

More laughter. "Go have some time to yourself, honey. I'll just work till my knees give out, then watch Netflix and chill."

"I don't think that means what you think it means, but okay, Mom. Love you."

"You too, honey."

After they hung up, she sat staring out the windshield for a long minute. She was so lucky to have such a great mom, and it always amused her when her momma pushed the limits with her speech or antics. But her mention of having a hot man made her feel like biting off all her nails.

She could open that file and find Shaw's address. She could go over there to see for herself that he was okay.

A case of the jitters hit and for a second, she bounced her knee and stared at the file as if it might combust right there on her passenger seat.

She brought a nail up to her teeth and nibbled the corner. "Dammit, Shaw. You leave me no choice."

Reaching over, she flipped open the file. There on the top was his name in Times New Roman font. Beneath that his age—32 and his sex M. As if one look at him didn't make a woman's ovaries explode with the knowledge that Shaw was *all* man.

She skimmed down to the address, and it gave the one on Bluebonnet Road and the farm where he'd grown up. Beneath that was another address, this one on the far end of the city. Atalee wasn't certain of how to get there, but after plugging it into her phone, her GPS app was calling out directions to her.

After a second of indecision, she flicked the file closed again so she wasn't tempted to read more. She already felt bad for digging too deep into Shaw's business, but he'd started it by coming to her—then disappearing.

As she navigated her way to the route, she felt an overwhelming draw to go to Shaw. Could it be there was enough of a bond between them that she was feeling him calling out to her? Anybody as entrenched in studies of the mind as she was would be laughing at her right now. If she ever admitted to another clinician that she believed in such nonsense, she'd be discredited in a hurry.

But she didn't believe in coincidence in cases like this. Shaw had come into her life for a purpose.

The sun was at the right angle to pierce her eyes, and she found her designer sunglasses and placed them on. It suddenly hit her that if she felt as young and carefree as her mother expected her to be, she'd be looking at this moment in a whole other light. It would be a fun time, driving to see her man.

Except Shaw wasn't her man, and there was a dark mystery surrounding him that she was half afraid to crack into.

To help him, she had to try, even if it meant that she'd be haunted by what she heard.

She stopped for gas and picked up a bottle of iced tea. Getting to the opposite side of the city took ages, especially in rush hour traffic on a Friday afternoon. By the time she reached Shaw's street, she was a mess of nerves.

The street looked like any other—normal houses with kids' toys littering front porches and planters full of flowers that looked about to expire in the heat of the afternoon. But one house flew the American flag, and her gaze locked on it.

She could still turn around, go home.

If she did, she'd hate herself.

He might not even be here.

She didn't want to consider what he was doing if not, so she stepped on the gas and rolled down the street. When she spotted the motorcycle tucked up next to the house beneath a carport, her heart gave a hard lurch.

Quickly, before she chickened out, she climbed from her car and stuffed the file into her handbag. The walk to his front door seemed like it was a mile long, even though it was only a few steps. She raised her fist and rapped on the wood door.

After a few seconds, she moved to knock again, when the door cracked.

"Jesus." Shaw's roughened tone hit her ears.

She ignored his reaction to seeing her on his doorstep and attempted a smile. "Nice place you have."

"It's a rental." He opened the door wider, and she saw his full body. Jeans slung low on his hips, his belt buckle bearing the name SHAW in finely etched letters. He was barefoot and bare-chested. But as her gaze lit on his chest, her knees threatened to buckle and it wasn't from desire.

He bore a scar down the center of his chest like that of a heart patient. Other scars dotted his chest and abdomen as well, but she couldn't take her gaze off the puckered line of skin that revealed just the edge of what Shaw had gone through in his life.

She'd missed it. She could have been there to support him, and she hadn't.

He noticed her staring at his chest and half-turned away. "What do you want?"

Oh boy. His question didn't sound all that friendly or inviting.

She flicked a look at his face. Mouth set in a straight line, brows slightly pinched over his deep blue eyes. He was hatless, his hair shorn shorter than she'd ever seen it.

"Shaw. Maybe I shouldn't have come, but..." She looked down at his long bare feet sprinkled with a

70

few dark hairs across the toes. Glancing up again, she said, "I had to make sure you're all right. You missed your last two appointments."

"I left a note with the receptionist that I could cancel."

"I know."

He contemplated her for so long that she began to think she should do an about-face and leave. He didn't want her bugging him, that was obvious.

"Maybe I should go," she said softly.

He pushed the door open farther and stepped back. "Come in, Atalee."

Her heart shouldn't give a sharp twist in her chest at the sound of her name on his lips, but she was helpless against it.

* * * * *

Fucking hell, Atalee was here—and his bed was two rooms away.

They didn't even need a bed—the wall was perfectly fine.

His cock had hardened at the first sight of her standing on his front walk, and now that she was inside his house, it was throbbing.

That indecision and worry on her face had been the deciding factor in letting her in. No, it was the sweet curve of her hips. No, her lips. Gawd, she was the whole package, and he wanted her with a ferocity that had brought bigger men than he was to their knees.

She stood awkwardly before him, and he raked his gaze over her appearance one more time. High heels in a nude pink color that had lewd thoughts swirling through his mind, a slim skirt ending at the most kissable of knees and another one of those sweaters. She must be dying in this heat, but he knew the longer sleeves were probably necessary in her air-conditioned office.

She swallowed and met his eyes.

Goddammit, he could not take her. He'd fucked up her life enough.

When her gaze skittered over his chest and scar a second time, his shoulders tensed. "Are you... all right?" she asked.

He gave a brisk nod and turned away to pick up his discarded T-shirt. As he slipped it over his head, she watched him. Damn, did she have to stand so close? All he had to do was snag her by the waist, lift her against his cock and claim her. The undressing would take care of itself.

He rubbed a hand over his head, wishing he had his hat so he could pull the brim low and escape those piercing sea-green eyes of hers.

Fuck-me eyes. Did she even realize how she was looking at him?

"Sit down." He waved at the sofa.

She did, sinking into one corner of the leather cushion and pulling a pillow onto her lap.

Don't do that, he wanted to say. *Don't hide from me.*

He took up the chair he favored, but it felt like sitting on springs and bolts when his mind was filled with thoughts of Atalee's soft form under him.

She let out a shaky breath. "I probably shouldn't have come, but I had to make sure you're all right."

"I am."

Her gaze dropped to his chest again, and he knew she was thinking of his scar. A leftover from his early days in the Texas Rangers.

While having her here was doing unspeakable things to his control, he'd just gotten in, showered the grime and most of the blood off himself, and thrown on a pair of jeans right after hearing the knock at the door. Even now, he could feel the fresh blood running down his calf from the wound on his leg.

The mission had been a bloody one, and he was damn lucky to have escaped with only this minor injury. He glanced down at his leg, and Atalee followed the action.

"You're bleeding!" She jumped up.

"Yeah, I was about to take care of it when you turned up."

"How can I help?"

A few drops of blood had hit the floor by his foot. "First-aid kit under the sink in the bathroom."

"I'll find it." She took off through his living room, sharp little heels tapping on the hardwood. Her curves disappeared around the corner, and Shaw leaned back in his chair, feeling the effects of twenty-four hours without sleep and a hell of a lot of physical exertion.

His eyes slipped closed, images of Atalee's round little ass flashing behind his lids before he heard the *tip-tap* of her return.

She was carrying the red box he'd used countless times over the past few months since joining the Ranger Ops. Or being recruited, rather.

Atalee knelt at his feet before he could stop her, and damn if his dick wasn't shoving hard at his fly now, aching with the need to sink into her wet mouth, pussy… or ass. If she'd let him.

God, he had to stop these thoughts before they got out of control.

He reached for the box. "I can do it."

"I'll help," she said at once. "It's your leg?"

He nodded and shifted to tug up his jeans over the bulge of his calf muscle. The ragged wound stung like hell, but all he could think about was Atalee kneeling at his feet. Dirtier thoughts than he'd ever had in his life popped into his mind.

She let out a low gasp at seeing his leg. "What happened to you?" she almost cried.

He latched his gaze onto hers. "Not the question to ask a man like me."

"It's a bullet wound, isn't it? Oh my God, Shaw!" As if to cover her reaction, she tore open the box lid and rifled through the contents.

"Gauze, alcohol, tape. That's all I need, baby doll." The endearment rolled off his tongue before he could snatch it back. She sat back on her heels and stared up at him, sea-green eyes burning with tears.

Jesus Christ, he was a goner for this woman.

Reaching out, he cupped her face in his palm, threading his fingers into her soft hair as he'd been wanting to forever.

"If you'll find me those items, I'll take care of it. No need to watch."

She shivered and leaned her head into his touch. Gawd, he couldn't stop this pull between them—it was like the tides.

"I-I'll help, I told you." Pulling away, she located the roll of gauze that was almost depleted from his last injury.

"Cut some into squares using those small scissors," he instructed.

She flashed a look at him. "How many times have you done this?"

He didn't answer—she didn't want to know.

He watched her snip the gauze into several squares. "That'll do," he said. Taking the bits, he pressed them to the wound, staunching the blood flow, which had slowed to a trickle. "If you'll cut a few more and pour some o' that alcohol on it, I'd appreciate it."

Without a word, she did as he asked, though she was a bit paler from the experience. He'd give her a nice shot of whiskey and get her feeling better.

Or two shots and make her clothes fall off.

He ground his teeth at the thought of her naked and spread-eagle on his bed.

"Are you sure you're ready for this? It's going to hurt," she said.

He gave a nod and removed the bloody bandage for her to clean the bullet graze, a good inch wide and half an inch deep, digging through the muscle of his calf.

When she pressed the alcohol-soaked gauze to the cut, he let out a hiss of pain. A tear dropped from her eye.

"Oh Jesus. Baby doll, I shouldn't have asked you to do this. Let me have it." He placed a hand over hers on his leg. Her hand shook, and she looked up at him, eyes swimming with tears.

"I'm okay. I just hate to hurt you, Shaw."

Hell, did she know how freakin' sweet she was? Probably not. Women like her were rare, because they did things for others without asking for anything in return. It was how he knew she was a great therapist.

"I'm okay," he assured her, though his tone took on his emotions and came out thick.

He took over for her, wiping harder to clean out the cut the way he knew she wouldn't for fear of hurting him further. "More gauze," he said.

When she handed it to him, he placed it beneath the wound and looked into her eyes. "Pour the alcohol straight in."

She shook her head. "I can't. It will hurt you."

"I have to clean it out, and it's too deep for just a wipe or two. Pour it in. Please, Atalee."

After two heartbeats, she nodded and picked up the bottle. It wavered over his leg, and then she dumped it.

The searing pain cut through his muscle, but he bit back any sounds he might have made if he was alone. When she looked up, he gave a nod to stop. "Now we just bandage it."

"That I can do. Lean back and let me take care of it."

He did, too tired to resist, and besides, having her soft hands working over his leg soothed him in ways he hadn't known he needed till now.

She fussed over him, placing the gauze bandage just so, and then she taped it down, commenting that the tape would pull out his leg hair when he removed it. That brought a half-smile to his lips. When she was finished, she sat back on her heels again.

That stirring was back full force, his cock head weeping pre-cum. Was it wrong of him to want to ask for a blow job?

He sat forward. "Thanks for your help."

"Of course." She got up and moved back to the sofa, though she didn't place the pillow over her lap this time. "Can I do anything else for you?"

He shook his head. "I just need sleep."

"Oh. I can go."

"Don't," he heard himself say, far grittier than he'd planned.

Her eyes widened in that innocent way they had on the day of her wedding when he'd lay his heart at her feet.

"We can talk a bit."

"If you're up to it." She bit into her lower lip, tugging at the skin and arousing the hell out of him.

They stared at each other. What was going through her mind? He'd like to know.

"As you can see, I'm fine."

"Except you've been shot at."

He chuckled. "Part of the job."

"You don't think anything of it, do you?" she asked with amazement in her voice.

"It's what I'm paid to do."

"It isn't about the money to you, so don't try to convince me it is."

The comfort of his chair—and her voice—were working magic on his exhausted being, and he felt himself sinking deeper into the cushions. "I doubt anyone who serves his country or the public does it for the money."

"Shaw, you're an amazing man, you know that?"

He shook his head. Lord, she was lovely, sitting there all prim and proper in her sweater and glasses, Ms. Clinical Psychologist. He'd like to bend her over and show her how a good, hard fucking could rock her world.

His eyes slipped shut.

Chapter Five

Watching Shaw sleep raised some deep, inner warmth in Atalee, wrapping around her heart like a soft blanket. After a few minutes, his breaths grew deep and even, and she knew he was out for the count.

Poor man must be dead tired to just drop off to sleep this way while talking to her. She glanced at his leg again, glad to see that no blood had seeped through the white of the gauze.

Quietly, she boxed up the first-aid kit and returned it to the bathroom, stealing away on her bare feet after kicking off her heels so as not to wake him. When she returned, her gaze roamed over him.

All steel and muscle, his expression stern enough to scare away anybody even in his dreams. For a moment, she stood watching him with indecision. Then she moved forward to pull the lever of the recliner, lowering the head and raising the footrest.

He didn't budge and his breathing never changed.

Feeling he was more comfortable, she looked at him again. She'd seen only a bit of him and the scars he bore were enough to make her heart tremble. How close had she come to losing him without even knowing it?

He also had a difficult time talking about himself, and now she knew what she had to do in order to truly help him.

She darted a look at her handbag, which held his file. On soft feet, she stole over to the sofa, grabbed the bag and headed to another room. She discovered his kitchen in such a neat state she wondered if he had a woman to clean up after him or if he hired someone. Either way, the idea gave her a pang.

She sank to a kitchen chair and took out the file. With it open on the warm, light wood tabletop and Shaw asleep in the other room, she began to read.

About ten o'clock, she stopped reading—there was a lot in here. Raising her head, she looked off toward the living room. The man had been through more shit than anybody should have lived through—and that was only as a Texas Ranger.

Now she knew what had caused that incision scar down his chest. It struck her that he wouldn't want her to know these things, so she couldn't bring it up to him or ever ask about the man who'd stabbed him in a vicious battle on the streets of Houston. The knife had slipped between Shaw's ribs and he'd collapsed. One of the other Texas Rangers on the scene had gotten him shuttled off to the hospital immediately, which had probably saved his life.

Turned out, that *was* an incision like a heart patient, because the knife had nicked Shaw's heart and they'd gone in to repair it.

He didn't seem the worse for it, though the entire thing made Atalee's blood run cold with fear for an event that had come and gone.

She wished she had been there to support him through it.

She shook her head. She couldn't think about that—she'd been married and had her own life to see to. There was little point in looking backward when Shaw was now in her present.

She got up, stretching out the kinks of hours spent hunched over his file. Drifting to the living room, she watched the beautiful man, his face softened as the restorative sleep healed him.

It was impossible to stay away from him. She walked over to the chair and trailed her fingers over his forearm, still hard and formidable even in a relaxed state.

He moved a bit under her touch. Then he grasped her by the arm and pulled her down. She hit his chest with what she felt was a hard thud, but he didn't even seem to wake.

Atalee went still. Was he aware he'd drawn her onto the chair with him? His breathing hadn't changed, which made her think he wasn't. Should she get up? Doing so might wake him, though.

And he felt nice beneath her. No, not nice — amazing. All hard and safe, his big chest cradling her and her hip perfectly fitted to his.

She breathed in and got a nose full of his fresh, soapy, masculine scent. Relaxing bit by bit, she lowered her ear to his chest and heard the solid drum of his heart. Another centimeter or two and Shaw would have been irreparable, but he'd been so damn lucky. Only a man like Shaw could use up some lives like a cat and live to tell — or not tell — about it all.

Her breathing matched itself to his and soon she was feeling drowsy. In his warm arms, she curled close and let her eyes slip shut.

If he woke and found her asleep on top of him, what would happen? Would he slide his hand up under her sweater and cup her breast, thumb the tip?

A shiver of excitement ran through her system. Call her wanton, but she hoped so.

* * * * *

The scents of frying eggs hit Shaw, and he cracked his eyes. Disoriented from sleep and from the lewd dreams he'd battled half the night, he finally realized he was in his recliner.

He moved a bit, feeling stiff after sleeping in a semi-upright position, though he'd found worse sleeping conditions in his life.

He blinked as it struck him — Atalee. She'd come to him last night, and she must be cooking eggs.

83

Wait a damn minute.

He sniffed his T-shirt. Sure enough, the soft notes of her perfume lingered on the fibers. Had she slept here with him in the recliner?

Now he was pissed—how the hell had he slept through such a thing? Finally having the woman of his dreams in his arms, tucked against what must have been one hell of nighttime boner knowing his dreams, and he hadn't even made his move.

He scrubbed a hand over his face. "Son of a bitch."

Getting up, he felt the twinge in his calf with every step he took toward the kitchen, but his libido—and his nose—carried him along. When he spotted Atalee, back to him and spatula in hand, he stopped dead.

Three pans were set on the burners of the stove, and judging by the scents, she had eggs, sausage and potatoes frying. Two plates were set out, and glasses of OJ had been filled.

God, she was cooking him a huge breakfast, and he didn't know if his stomach, his heart or his cock was more affected.

At the scuff of his bare foot on the floor, she tossed a glance over her shoulder. A smile lit her face. "Morning, sunshine. You slept like a log."

He hoped he hadn't snored.

"God, that looks good."

She faced him.

He didn't mean the food cooking on the stove.

Even in her wrinkled skirt and sweater from the previous day, her hair unbrushed and tousled, she was glorious.

And exactly what he wanted to open his eyes to every damn day of his life from here forward.

"Have some juice," she said, waving toward the glasses.

He reached around her, purposely brushing close, and closed his fingers around his glass. He brought it to his lips and chugged the entire thing in seconds. When he slammed it back down on the counter, her mouth dropped open, but he didn't give her time to think about what he would do next.

Grabbing her, he hitched her against him—hard. As he lowered his mouth to hers, he felt a shudder race through her body. "I've wanted to do this for years," he grated out a split second before he claimed her lips.

She made a sound of surrender as he angled his head and deepened the kiss. The pressure of his hand on her spine bowed her to him, and her perky breasts pushed upwards against his chest.

Jesus, why the hell hadn't he done this years ago? She was sweet heaven.

Lashing her to him, he lifted her onto tiptoe as he pushed his tongue into her mouth. The first sweep was bliss—the second shook his control. Atalee raised her hands to his chest, clinging to his shoulders as he bent to his task.

Tasting her bit by bit, sinking deeper with every pass of his tongue. As he finally got to slip his hand under her hair and feel the blonde silk flow over the backs of his fingers, he hardened to full mast. All the pressure of his night of passionate dreams featuring this beauty right here in his arms had him biting back his need to explode.

He yanked back and stared into her eyes, gauging her reaction to him. If he hadn't tasted her desire on her tongue, he saw it in those crystalline eyes.

He slammed his mouth over hers again. When he felt her fingers fumble over his back, he battled with an inner need that went far beyond what he'd ever dreamed it could.

Lifting her, he spun to the counter, settling her on the top and cupped the back of her head as he swooped in for another round at those tormenting lips.

She stopped him with a hand on his chest. "The food will burn."

He reached over and switched off all three burners with a flick of his wrist. "To hell with the food. I've got something tastier right here." He took her mouth again, this time showing her how damn serious he was about having her.

All of her.

Parting her thighs, he wedged his body between them and thrust his tongue deep into her mouth. She gulped back a sexy cry and settled her hands on his chest.

He was well aware of the second she laid eyes on his scar peeking from the neck of his shirt, and he watched her carefully as she traced a fingertip down his front.

"Does it hurt?" she whispered.

"No. Just a battle scar."

To his shock, she moved in slowly and pressed a delicate kiss to the top and began working her way down it. With each soft caress of her lips, he lost himself a little more to this woman. This delicious, perfect girl who was now free from her marriage, in his kitchen... and about to be fucked like she'd never been fucked before.

* * * * *

Atalee's panties were ruined, soaked through with juices of her arousal, and she was too far gone to think of Shaw being her patient. After this, she was totally certain they couldn't work together in that capacity, and while she wanted to help him in any way possible, she was just fine with that.

She dug her fingers into his hard shoulders even as she traced the line of his scar downward with gentle kisses. Passion flowed through her veins until she couldn't think of anything but taking off her clothes.

Just as she thought she might expire from her own need, she raised her head and found Shaw's intense stare on her.

Without a word, he tore open her cardigan. A pearl button went flying and her bra followed. When he cupped both her breasts and dipped his head to kiss and suck her nipples, moving between them like a starving man, she tossed back her head and gave in to the moans falling from her lips.

Liquid heat pooled low in her belly, and she wiggled closer. Suddenly, he picked her up and spun again, this time, swiping an arm over the mail piled up on the table and scattering it to the four corners of the kitchen as he set her down hard.

Their gazes locked, and she lunged upward for him, arms looped around his neck as he attacked her skirt, hitching it up and somehow getting it around her waist.

"Gawd, you're sexy as hell." He bit into her lower lip with a tenderness that was shocking coming from a man as big and lethal as Shaw was. But when he cupped her pussy in one hand as if he owned it, she stopped thinking and let her body take over.

"Take me, Shaw," she begged, going for his belt. She'd awakened with that buckle digging into her side and a glance in the bathroom mirror showed the red outline of a corner, a sleep dent she didn't mind one bit.

It felt like a brand.

He closed his lips around her nipple and sucked with long pulls while teasing her clit through the cloth of her panties. She shimmied closer, urging him to really touch her. To finally touch her.

Each stroke over the crotch of her panties had her need amping up higher, growing hotter. She felt like she rode the rim of a volcano and was more than willing to leap into the molten fire as long as Shaw took her there.

When he hooked his finger into her panties and yanked them aside, he swayed back to look at her.

All of her.

"You're freakin' soaked." He pressed her backward onto the table so she had to plant her hands behind her to brace herself, and he ripped her panties off her ankles. As he stared into her eyes, he reached for his belt buckle.

Watching this huge, gorgeous man undress for her had been the stuff of her fantasies, and now it was a reality. Only there was no bed, only a kitchen table, and hell if she cared.

She watched him unbuckle his belt and the gold bar bearing his name flick aside. The top button popped open and he lowered the zipper with an easy grace that belied his size. She suddenly imagined those nimble fingers working over some intricate wires of a bomb or feeding bullets into a weapon.

She slammed the door on those thoughts and focused on Shaw. He reached into his boxers and pulled out a cock so long, thick and impressive that she swallowed a gasp. The shock of seeing how amazing he was right to the mushroomed tip had her panting with lust.

Letting her legs fall apart, she beckoned him to come to her.

His eyelids lowered over his smoldering irises. He stepped up to the side of the table and grasped her by the hips. "I hope to hell you're on birth control, because this is happening with nothing between us."

Staring at his thick cock burrowing between her thighs was enough to steal her senses, and he pinched her chin lightly between thumb and forefinger, raising her gaze to his. "Baby doll. Are you safe?"

"Yes." The lines between caring and not caring blurred.

"Me too," he ground out as he tugged her across the table to the very edge — to the tip of his cock.

He held her eyes and threaded their fingers before moving another inch. "If this happens, we can't go back."

"I don't care — I want it." She hooked her hand around his neck and yanked him in.

He filled her in one slick, long, hard, stretching glide.

She cried out, and he slammed his mouth across hers, stealing the sound even as he grunted out one of his own.

God, he was huge, filling her—overfilling her. She looked up at him, noting the strain around his eyes and cutting lines at the corners of his mouth. His eyes were a deeper blue than ever, and her heart—already his—tumbled headlong.

Testing her limits, she rocked her hips upward. He let out a groan and pierced her in his gaze. "Next time I'm eating your pussy until you can't quit screaming."

"You'd better live up to your promises, Woody." His nickname brought a quirk to his lips.

"They don't call me that for nothin'."

"Let your hips do the talkin'." Burning with desire, she pushed up against him, forcing him to move.

As each inch of his cock left her body, she felt a sizzling heat envelop her. Staring into her eyes, he drove back in, stretching her once again.

"Oh God, Shaw. Don't stop." She'd never pleaded in her life, but right now, she had no shame. She was mostly naked on his kitchen table while the breakfast she'd cooked cooled in the pans on the stove, and all she wanted was to come around him, squeezing him so hard that it forced him to shake apart in her arms.

With a growl, he captured her mouth, swiping his tongue over hers five times, six, while plunging into her body. His muscles flexed under her hands, and his scents surrounded her. As he sank to her deepest point, she felt the first flutters of her orgasm rushing up.

Her insides clamped down. He bit off a moan and churned his hips faster. The table rocked on its legs, but she wasn't afraid of it breaking, because if it did she knew Shaw would catch her before she hit the floor and probably continue fucking her at the same time.

He *was* a superhero, after all.

Her inner walls clenched. Released. Clenched once more. Her small cries grew louder, and soon it was too much. She crested that pinnacle and dove down the other side of the steep slope, her juices squeezing from her pussy as he pumped in and out of her.

"Hell!" He arched his neck, giving her a view of the cords standing out. He tensed in her hold and the first spurt of white-hot cum hit her insides.

The moment turned from desperate to tender in a blink, as Shaw collapsed forward, his forehead pressed to hers and his eyes bright with pleasure as he drained his release into her. His lips found hers, and their tongues tangled in a long, deep kiss that lasted until the final jet left his body and her contractions faded away.

A heartbeat passed. Atalee pushed Shaw back enough to look into his eyes.

"I'm not fucking done with you," he grated out. Gathering her to his chest, he drew her upright as he dragged his jeans and boxers up enough to walk. Then before she could hop off the table, he yanked her into his arms.

Every step to his bedroom felt like thunder passing through her body. When he nudged open his door and strode into the space, she leaned her head against his chest and listened to his strong heartbeat.

He lay her down on his bed. While he'd slumbered this morning, she'd explored the house and had found this space spare, minimal and masculine. All the things she thought of when she thought of Shaw Woodward.

The only thing she hadn't seen before was a handgun in its holster laying atop his light wood dresser. It spoke of things she didn't understand about him but wanted to find out. She hoped in time he would open up to her and let her know why he'd come to the VA hospital seeking help.

After he laid her down, he pushed to a stand again and stripped out of his jeans and boxers, letting them drop to the floor. She reached beneath herself and fought to find the zipper on her skirt, but Shaw's sure fingers met hers and he got the zipper down and her skirt off as well.

They stared at each other, both naked, both still panting from their shared release just seconds before and the force of wanting more.

His eyes began his lovemaking before he even placed a hand on her. Roaming over her hair to her collarbones and down to her breasts, that pinched in arousal at his gaze. Then he skimmed over the flat of her belly, bearing a little extra weight from stress eating following her marriage breakup. He didn't seem to mind and gave a hungry growl as he landed on the triangle of dark blonde curls covering her mound.

She hadn't bothered to lady-scape in ages—who was she supposed to look good down there for? Again, he didn't mind.

As he grasped her by the knees and parted her thighs, she let out a rasp of need.

"These curls are sopping wet for me." He dragged a fingertip through the damp curls on her outer lips.

Before she knew his intention, he laid down between her legs, thumbed apart her folds and licked her.

Licked their combined release without batting an eye.

This man was dirty and hot and all the things she wanted rolled into one. She couldn't tear her gaze away from Shaw's long tongue moving up and down her seam and circling her hard clit. The ache in her tripled, and she had no idea where her body ended and his mouth began. She didn't care, because she was so close to coming again.

He slid one hand under her ass, lifting her to his feasting mouth—and simultaneously drove two fingers into her pussy.

She couldn't stop her cries this time, each louder than the next. She thrashed under him, bucking to take everything he'd give and demanding more, more, more. His blue eyes burned from between her thighs as he placed a slow lick from bottom to top and then sucked her nubbin. The way he stroked her inner wall with his fingers too...

"Oh my God, Shaw!"

He rumbled against her pussy, almost urging her to peak for him.

It took her five seconds flat. Fisting the sheets, she rocked in rhythmic time to his tongue and fingers, her body humming so loud she couldn't even hear her own voice calling out his name.

* * * * *

Shaw took his cock in hand, harder than it had been before his release, and fed it inch by inch into Atalee's tight sheath. She clutched at him with her walls, tightening as he seated himself deep within her.

The flavors of them both were on his tongue, fueling his lust. And the look of pure bliss on her beautiful face made him want to do a victory lap around the house.

He'd given her two orgasms before breakfast and he didn't know if he could stop at a third. Now that he had her in his bed, he wasn't letting her out till they both collapsed.

Or he got called out with Ranger Ops. He hoped to hell not, but shit was still brewing with that group, and he felt like it was just the tip of the iceberg.

He withdrew and spent some time teasing his swollen cock head up and down her pussy before angling it and sinking in again. She caught his hand and held it fast, which only bound him to her more. Their link—he'd fucking known it was there from the beginning, goddammit—was strong and alive. He sank in again and lost himself in the sensation of her lips on his, skating over his jaw to his neck and her wet, hot pussy enveloping him.

The time between her long-ago wedding day had now faded in a blink of pleasure as he brought her off again. His own release lay like a coiled snake at the base of his spine, so close. One more plunge would do him in. Then she reached up and pinched his nipples, and his body seized in a bliss that made his jaw clench tight on a roar.

Pumping his hot cum into her body a second time was too much. He had to say it.

"I never stopped wanting you."

She wrapped her arms and legs around him, holding him tight as he folded on top of her. He lasted a minute there before she grunted at his weight. With a chuckle, he rolled off, drawing her with him into a curled position he suspected was like the one they'd slept in.

When she walked her fingers over his chest, he caught her hand, holding it tight. "You really are good at therapy, baby doll."

She giggled, burying her face against his shoulder. "At least I have something to show for a hundred grand in student loans."

They shared a laugh, and the sound of his stomach rumbling with hunger was heard over it. Atalee tipped her head to look up at him. "I'll heat up that breakfast again."

He kissed the top of her head. "Two orgasms and a big breakfast. Must be my lucky day."

Chapter Six

The minute Atalee's mother set eyes on her, she gave Atalee that look that told her she knew something was going on. It could be mother's instinct, but Atalee figured it was the fact she couldn't stop smiling.

"You seem to be in a chipper mood," her momma commented.

"I am." She immediately dug into the task of sorting out old handbags. She held up one that was surely from 1983. "Didn't you ever throw anything away?"

"You know how styles come back in."

"Not this." She tossed the teal purse into the donation box and had rummaged through four or five more, when her mother spoke again.

"Did you have some of that fun I told you to have yesterday?"

How to answer this? Her mother didn't really want to hear details, only that Atalee was happy.

She nodded and left it at that. Together, they sat cross-legged on the floor sorting through box after box of handbags, scarves and shoes. When the final box was pushed aside, her mother flopped back on the floor in her usual melodramatic fashion.

"You *are* a slave driver, Atalee. I thought I raised you to be much lazier."

"That was only my teen years."

Her mother tossed an old slipper that had seen better days at her, and Atalee scooped that up and dumped it into the trash box too.

She stood back to survey the room while her mom rolled over to get up and stand beside her. The bookcases were now empty, awaiting books and baskets. The closet was in order, with clothing hanging in the color order of the rainbow.

"Looking good in here. So was it Shaw?"

Atalee stared at her. "You ask those two unrelated questions as if they're part of the same conversation. Really, they're not even in the same zip code."

Her momma grinned. "Well?"

Atalee had no reason to lie. "Yes, it was Shaw."

"I knew it by the spark in your eyes that you'd been with that man."

"How could you possibly know by a look that it was Shaw?" Her tone took on one of teasing, but Atalee was interested to know if she wore her happiness on the outside. The morning with Shaw had been incredible, and her body felt the effects of his strong fingers, lips… and cock.

"You have the same expression this morning as you did when you mentioned him to me before. Now, should we take a break till tomorrow?"

Atalee laughed. "You're not getting off the hook so easily. We're close to finishing this whole room, Mom!"

She gave Atalee a flat look. "Are we even standing in the same room, honey? We have another week ahead of us just to put things away.

"All the more reason to start on it now."

"Honey, you need to get a dog or something to fill your time. This organization fever in you isn't healthy. I'm going to get us some sweet tea." Without another word, her momma strode from the room, leaving Atalee shaking her head. If she didn't know her mother as she did, she'd wonder if their roles had reversed and she'd become the parent.

She grabbed one of the new baskets they'd purchased with small compartments to separate makeup and set it on a stack of boxes. Then she began stashing mascara, lipstick and blusher into their own areas. When her momma returned with sweet tea in hand, Atalee held up the basket.

"See how nice?"

"Yes, it's lovely. Here's your tea." They stood sipping for a moment.

"So are you seeing Shaw this evening too?"

She nearly choked on the swallow of tea she was taking. "You're relentless, Momma."

"I know somebody just like that." She gave her a pointed look.

"All right, I admit to that much, but I refuse to own up to an unhealthy organization fever. No, I'm not seeing Shaw tonight. He had something to do."

Her mom made a sound in her throat.

"What's that for?" Atalee asked, fiddling with a strand of hair that wouldn't stay out of her eyes.

"It means I approve of taking things slowly," she said.

Atalee set aside her tea and folded her arms over her chest. "You approve of going slowly when you're the one who pushed me to go have fun. I don't know how to interpret any of this, Mom."

"Honey, you just got out of a nasty marriage and a divorce. I want you to have fun, but just go slow and find your footing. There's no rushing required here."

Atalee nodded at once. Her momma was right— except she didn't know the entire story about how she'd spent a lot of time thinking about Shaw and being with him overnight had solidified the idea in her mind that he really was as awesome as her imagination had guessed at.

Her momma didn't have a clue how deep Atalee felt after being in Shaw's arms, with his cock moving inside her and his beard burn on her inner thighs.

Grabbing her tea again, she hid her expression by sipping.

101

"Uh-oh." Her momma gave her that look.

The one that told Atalee she was found out, and nothing she could do or say would conceal how she felt from the woman who'd birthed her.

"I'm not ready to talk about it, please."

"Whenever you're ready."

She stared at her mother hard. "If you think you can pick at me till I tell you something, you're wrong. I'm a woman now, not a five-year-old."

"All right, honey." She patted her arm and moved to one of the boxes to get to work.

Suddenly, Atalee realized where she'd gotten her ability to read people and get them to open up and talk to her about their problems. She'd received that gene from her mother, and damn if she didn't want to have her own therapy session right now.

No, she had some sorting of her own to do first— in her mind and heart. *Momma's right—take things slow.*

* * * * *

"Can I get another beer?" Nash said to the waitress. He looked to Shaw. "You?"

"I'm good, thanks."

The waitress smiled at both of them before moving away from their table. Neither watched her leave.

102

"Okay, what the hell's up with you, man?" Nash cocked his brow.

Shaw looked at him in surprise. "Whattaya mean?"

"I mean"—he spread his hands on the tabletop, showing no less than two cuts and a bite mark resulting from their last mission— "you don't want a second beer and you're not eyeing up pretty waitresses after they've practically jumped into your lap."

Shaw shook his head. "Not interested in the beer or the woman."

"And that's because...?"

"Just feelin' a bit different is all."

Nash reached across the table and tapped Shaw's temple. He moved back in surprise. "What's that for?"

"Tryin' to see if you got a soft spot from that blast you took back on the border."

"No, but my calf still stings like a bitch." Shaw lifted his jaw toward Nash. "I hope you got a tetanus shot after that son of a bitch bit you."

"Already had one. Nevaeh wasn't very happy, though."

Shaw almost said he knew the feeling, since Atalee had actually welled up with tears at the sight of his bullet graze.

"So what's different?" Nash asked just as the waitress hustled back with hips swaying to set his beer before him.

She dropped a sideways look at Shaw. "Sure I can't get you anything?"

"No thanks."

She smiled and turned to go, this time with a bit less bounce in her step.

Nash picked up his draft. "You could at least smile at her."

Shaw lifted a French fry from his plate and bit into it. "Like I said, not feelin' it."

"I respect that. Anyway, is there a reason why you called me for lunch today?" Nash sipped his beer and swiped some foam off his upper lip.

Shaw swallowed his fry. "I wanted to tell you that I found a shrink."

Nash sat back in his chair and nodded. "Glad to hear it. Hope it's workin' out for you."

A grin spread over Shaw's face against his will as thoughts of what his pretty little therapist had done with him all morning long. Even after the big breakfast she'd cooked, he'd dragged her to the shower and worked soap all over her—and his cock into her.

"That's it, man. What the fuck's going on with you?" Nash set down his glass.

Shaw leaned forward. "Ever had kitchen table sex?"

104

Nash barked out a laugh that had several heads whipping their direction. Both of them ignored the onlookers and shared a long chuckle. Slapping the table with his palm, Nash said, "I knew somethin' was up." His face changed, and he went dead still.

That was when Shaw felt his own pocket vibrate with an incoming call.

"Dammit to hell." Nash went for his phone but Shaw already had his in hand. They were on their feet in a flash, and Shaw threw some bills on the table to cover the tab while Nash booked it for the door.

On the street, they wove through pedestrians to reach their vehicles. Shaw wished he didn't have his motorcycle, so they could make better time in rallying to meet the other Ranger Ops.

As Shaw reached his bike and threw a leg over it, he met Nash's gaze. "The fuckin' governor—did I hear that right?"

"Yeah. See ya at the base."

The home base for the Ranger Ops was nothing more than a government office where they were given orders or debriefed, and it was a running joke that it was so low budget because Homeland Security didn't want to put money into the Ranger Ops anyway.

Shaw hit the streets, quickly moving around some slower vehicles. He ran a red light and set a faster pace. A threat to the governor wasn't unheard of. As a Texas Ranger, he'd been called out to protect one political figurehead or another over the past few years, but it must be bigger and more serious if Ranger Ops was called in.

He arrived at the rallying point before Nash did, parked his bike and walked over to Linc and Lennon, who were climbing out of a car.

Shaw grabbed his phone and checked if more information had come in, but his screen was blank. "Let's go." As second in command, he took control by leading his teammates into the building. While they went straight to their row of lockers and began suiting up, Cavanagh came in and got to business checking weapons and ammo. Jess and Nash entered last, and Nash braced his legs wide as he filled them in on everything he knew.

Threat. Check.

Keeping the governor under guard. Check.

His teenage son was also in the mix, believed to be in custody of a terrorist group acting against the governor.

Shaw slipped his bulletproof vest over his head. "How do we know the son isn't involved in the group for his own reasons?"

"We don't." Nash looked at Shaw closely. "You good for this, Woody?"

He grunted, half pissed off that Nash would even question whether or not he could perform his fucking job. "I got it."

Nash gave a hard nod and strapped his weapon to his hip. "You assholes got one minute to load up."

"Guts 'n glory, man," Jess called out to Nash's back.

Shaw let Nash's question sink in. *Was* he good? He was about to find out.

* * * * *

Something was very, very wrong. Shaw, the man who had touched Atalee so thoroughly just a few days before, sat upright on the sofa in her office, staring straight ahead. Even without schooling, she would know something was wrong by the way he seemed to be watching something play in his head.

She knew better than to break into such a moment, yet Shaw hadn't moved in almost five minutes, and her worry was mounting by the second.

When he'd shown up in her office out of the blue, she'd been surprised to say the least. And after their encounter, it had become quite apparent to him that she could not treat him as a patient. Yet when he'd walked in with that haunted look in his eyes, how could she turn him away?

She had to speak. "Shaw," she said quietly. They'd both agreed she should not treat him as a patient, yet how could she turn him away when he'd shown up at her door?

He didn't look around at her, but he *did* blink. It was a start.

"Shaw, can you start by telling me the first emotion in your mind?"

Swinging his head to her, he pierced her in his gaze—his very lucid gaze. "I don't operate that way, Atalee."

Okay. She took another tack. "You came here to talk. It must mean you trust me to hold those confidences."

After long seconds, he gave a nod. "I trust you."

A flutter hit her belly. "I appreciate that."

Suddenly, he heaved himself off the couch and walked to the window that looked out on the parking lot. With his arms folded and his back rigid, she didn't know if she was getting a single word out of the man today. Problem was, she knew him, yet she didn't. Knew enough to understand he was struggling with some issue and not enough to have a clue how to help him.

"Have you ever looked at the world out there and wondered how the hell people are happy?" he asked.

Treading carefully, she remained seated rather than going to him as her gut told her to. "I know a lot of bad things happen to people and I do sometimes marvel that the world seems to go on anyway."

He nodded. "Exactly." He pointed. "Take that guy there for instance. He doesn't walk hunched over with the weight of the world on his shoulders. He looks relatively normal, adjusted, content."

Oh boy.

She got to her feet and moved toward him. His scent hit her first, masculine and plucking at her

108

nerve endings like no other man in her life ever had. Looking at his broad shoulders, she wondered what kind of weights bore down on him.

When she set her hand on his shoulder, he turned to her and grasped her by the elbows. She felt the heat of his hands sink through the fibers of her blouse and travel all over her body in a shorter time than it took her to blink.

His blue eyes burned into hers. "Let's get outta here."

Her lips fell open. "Where?"

"Take a ride. Anywhere. Can you leave?"

"You're my last patient." Actually, her last patient had gone long ago, and she'd just been attempting to finally clean off her desk when the receptionist had come in all atwitter to tell Atalee that Shaw was here.

"Let's go." He started to the door, pulling her along in his wake.

"Wait, I need my handbag."

He paused, and she went back to fetch it from behind her desk. When she threw a forlorn glance at the pile of work laying there—notes to jot down, dictation to take on the latest patients—Shaw cupped her chin in his big palm and stared into her eyes.

"I need you," he grated out.

Her heart turned over. "Let's go." *I'm yours,* she wanted to add but refrained. This wasn't about them right now—it was about Shaw getting his thoughts and emotions in some semblance of order so he could go on in a healthy manner.

At the door of her office, she pulled free of his grasp. "We can't be seen together this way. Go on and I'll catch up with you."

Understanding had his eyes clearing somewhat, as he came back to reality. "Of course. Don't be long."

After he walked out the door, why did she regret not taking hold of him, drawing him close and letting him know that everything was going to be all right? She quivered on the other side of the door for several minutes before following.

All the way down in the elevator, she let her nerves kick in. Was she doing the right thing by Shaw? He needed therapy, not a lover. She could lose her position for this and her reputation would forever be stained.

Yet, when he pulled up in his car and reached across the center to open the door for her, she couldn't have stopped herself from climbing in with him if she'd tried.

They drove for a minute before she spoke. "I didn't know you still had this car." It was the topic of many of his and Johnny's conversations, as he'd been rebuilding it at the time. A classic car from the sixties that was much coveted by some of the guys who knew him.

"Wouldn't let this baby go." The way he caressed the steering wheel had her aching to be the leather beneath his hand. Those long fingers had given her more pleasure than her fantasies had ever relayed.

She shifted in her seat, and his gaze shot to her.

"I can't talk back there, Atalee. It's not me."

"I know."

"I know you read my file."

Fuck. Her heart lurched, and she dropped her stare to her hands. "I'm sorry."

"At least you know some."

"Yes."

"But not all."

She studied his profile, the tic in his jaw and the way his pulse beat erratically in his throat. "Not all," she echoed softly, reaching across the space to touch his hand, an iron grip on the wheel now.

He gave it to her, letting her mesh their fingers on the console between them. He swallowed hard. "I killed a child."

His abrupt words sent her into a shocked whirlwind. She couldn't even blink. "A... child? In the line of duty?"

"We were protecting the fucking governor two days ago. Death threats, fucking unmarked packages they believed were bombs being delivered. You know his stance on gun control, right?"

She nodded. It was a wonder the man hadn't been targeted before now. He was pretty unpopular at this stage of the game.

"Yeah, there's a group we've heard murmurings from before. Knight Ops dealt with some of their shit a few months back, but this was our first encounter with them."

She rolled with the information he threw at her. Though she had no clue who Knight Ops was, she could guess it was another special ops force.

Shaw shook his head as if casting away some heavy yoke thrown over his neck. "Never should have gotten that far."

His fingers tightened around hers, and she stroked the back of his hand with her free one. "Shaw, you do what you're told."

"No, I fucking don't." His voice came out as mechanical, and it scared her, lifting the hairs on her arms.

"Can you tell me more?" she prompted, afraid if she let him sink too far into his head that he wouldn't come back to her. He seriously needed help, and she wasn't enough, not when they were too close already.

"In Mexico, shit went down and it's affecting me." He took his hand off the wheel long enough to tap the center of his head.

So what had happened recently wasn't directly related, just an aftereffect of some trauma he'd experienced in Mexico. None of which was in his file. At least not any file she could get her hands on.

"Shaw. Why don't you pull over here and we'll talk? Look, there's a park and we can walk on the path."

"Jesus Christ." His words were more like his own, but her insides shook to think of what was happening and how she could help *right now* when he needed her the most.

"Pull in right here." She pointed and he did.

When he came to a stop, he turned to her. "I'm sorry."

"That's why I'm here, Shaw. If you can tell me more, we can figure out a plan to get you the help you need."

He grabbed her and dragged her across the seat into his lap. She fell with a soft thump onto his very hard thighs, and before she could draw a breath of his manly scent, he tipped her face up to his with his thumb under her chin.

Staring deep into her eyes, he grated out, "All I know is when I look in your eyes, I see why the people are happy."

He kissed her.

* * * * *

Every demon chasing through Shaw's mind got shoved behind a closed door the instant his mouth touched Atalee's. She melted into his touch, breasts pressed to his chest and her arms spun around his neck, clinging to him as he slanted his mouth for more.

He dragged his lips away and dropped his forehead to hers, panting with the balls-out urge to take her right here on public park lands. A second ticked by, and she drew her hand down to his nape, her touch soft and sure.

"Shaw, this thing between us is strong, but I think you need to talk more."

He nodded, nose brushing against hers.

She shifted in his lap as if to move back to her seat. Locking his hands on her hips, he said, "Don't move."

"If you're sure you can think this way, but I—"

"No, there's a man at the window. Don't move out of my lap. Get my gun tucked in my waist along my spine."

Her blood ran cold as she realized what he was telling her to do. She'd never touched a gun in all her life, and she hoped he wasn't going to order her to fire it, because no way in hell could she.

Or maybe she could—under extreme circumstances. If it meant either of their lives, she could pull the trigger.

With fear pounding in her veins, she slowly slipped her hand down his shoulder, along his hard torso until she reached his hip and around his back. The steel under her hand scared the bejeezus out of her.

"Pretend you're kissing me," he told her. "And put the gun into my hand."

Swallowing hard, she tipped her mouth up to his. He brushed his lips across hers, still tender despite the situation they found themselves in. Working the gun from the holster, her heart drummed so heavily she thought she might pass out.

When his fingers curled around the weapon she held, things happened fast and in a blur. He grabbed her and shoved her down and away from him even as he exploded out of the driver's door. She couldn't see what was going on, and she had to make sure he was okay.

Launching out the door after him, she saw Shaw standing with his legs braced wide and weapon trained on a guy who also held a gun.

"Let's play a game of Russian roulette, why don't we?" Shaw drawled out at the man. "You take a shot and I take a shot to see which one of us actually has a loaded weapon."

The guy danced from foot to foot. "Give me your money and credit cards."

"Why don't you go fuck yourself? Or better yet, get clean and find a job that doesn't involve ambushing people getting out of their cars at a park. Now"—his finger twitched on the trigger— "about that Russian roulette."

Atalee could barely hear their voices above the pounding of her heart. She stood close to Shaw, but he didn't flick his gaze away from his adversary. He did, however, move his leg ever so slightly, blocking her.

No wonder the man was riddled with scars. He'd take a bullet for her, probably had taken some for others.

Her love bloomed, sprouting several dozen more flowers in the bouquet inside her heart.

Shaw made a sudden, sharp move, and in the next second, she saw the gunman on the ground, disarmed, with his arm jerked up and back at an angle that wasn't human.

He bellowed with pain, but Shaw didn't flinch. He held his gun on the man with a mask of indifference on his face. "Baby doll, get my phone off the dash and dial the number six."

With shaking hands, she reached for it. Pressing the number got dicey when a tremor of terror racked her, but she managed to bring the phone to her ear as well.

"What the hell's going on, Woody?"

Woody... the man on the other end of the line was addressing Shaw.

"Uhh... it's not Woody, but he told me to call."

"Goddammit. What's your location?"

Thank goodness she knew exactly where they were, having hiked here many times during the cooler winter months. She spouted it off, and the man grated out, "I'll be there in five. Tell him not to shoot anybody unless he has to."

Her mind blanked on what to say in return, but he ended the call.

Two young men came across the parking lot, shooting interested looks their way.

"Get in your truck and don't think about this," Shaw ordered.

They ducked their heads and ran the rest of the way to their truck. The man on the ground still howled intermittently in pain, and no wonder—that dislocated shoulder must be excruciating. Shaw had zero sympathy, though, and stood over him with all the authority of a man who did this for a living.

God, he was hot.

Atalee was too afraid to think much more. What seemed like an hour went by. When a black SUV hit the parking lot, Shaw raised his gaze to Atalee. "That's my backup. Sit tight while we sort this motherfucker, okay?"

She gave a jerky nod and looked on in shock as a huge man climbed from the SUV along with another and another. These three men, along with Shaw, looked as if they could subdue ISIS with a single glare.

Shaw's friend stopped before the one on the ground and drawled, "Nice dislocation we have here. Take much?"

Shaw shook his head. "The usual."

The usual? Oh God, how often did something like this happen? She didn't want to know.

She stood with as much dignity as a woman could who'd nearly been ravished and then shoved into a ball on the floor to stay out of harm's way. One of the guys looked at her.

"You okay, honey?" he asked, low, probably so as not to scare her further.

She nodded.

"Weapon's not even loaded," Shaw told the massive man beside him.

Struck with the realization that he hadn't been calling the man's bluff, she said, "H-how did you know?"

Shaw's gaze lit on her, making her feel warm and protected even from several paces away. "It's a known fact that many armed robbers don't even have bullets in their weapons."

So he didn't truly know but had guessed. She didn't know whether to think *damn, he's good* or run for the hills. This man was a harder version of himself from the old days. Changed.

She couldn't imagine the things he'd done in his lifetime that he hadn't even confessed to her. Honestly, it terrified her to think of.

In the back of her mind, she heard her momma's voice, asking if she was still up to the challenge.

She was.

Lifting her chin a notch, she looked at the man who seemed to be leading this show. "I'm Atalee."

"Nash," he grated out. "Want to give me your statement?"

One of the guys chuckled.

"She doesn't have to do that," Shaw said.

"You know protocol. We gotta get it from another perspective, if there is one."

She nodded to Shaw, and he gave the slightest nod. Nash took her arm and moved her back to sit in the open doorway in the driver's seat. He crouched before her. Behind him, the guys picked up the gunman with the dislocated shoulder. She couldn't see how they handled him, but he screamed in pain all the way to the back of the SUV.

She looked up at Nash. Under his cowboy hat, his eyes were dark and in shadow but not unkind. "W-what will you do with him?"

"Drop him at the emergency room and then he'll be escorted to the county jail for assault with a weapon and attempted robbery. You okay, Atalee? Can I get you a water or something?"

"No, I'm okay."

Shaw was back, standing over Nash's shoulder, listening to every word as Nash asked what had taken place. She paused to ask if he needed to write this down, he smiled and tapped his temple.

When she got to the part where Shaw had told her to pretend to kiss him, Nash tossed a look back over his shoulder.

"Sounds familiar. Who knew it was one of your regular ploys?"

To her surprise, out of nowhere, Shaw's hard expression splintered into a grin so wide and beautiful it would make any woman around him fall to her knees and beg.

"It worked well before. Figured it would work again," he said.

Nash chuckled and returned to questioning Atalee. Once the rest of the story was out, he nodded and pushed to his feet. Shaw butted him out of the way and reached into the car for Atalee. She placed her hands in his and he drew her into his arms, head bowed to her hair, rocking her lightly in a way that made her think of slow dancing.

"We got this handled, Woody. Guts 'n glory." Nash headed to his vehicle.

"Guts 'n glory," Shaw called after him. Then he tipped up Atalee's face to his. Searching her eyes, he said, "Where were we?" And kissed her.

Chapter Seven

Shaw walked Atalee to her front door and watched her open it with a key. She pushed open the door and looked back at him.

"Come in," she said quietly.

Hell, he'd scared the shit out of her and it was a miracle she wasn't shoving him away from her.

He caught her gaze, held it. "You sure?"

"Yes." To prove it, she took his hand and pulled him inside. He closed the door and locked it.

They stared at each other. "I'd like to change," she said.

He nodded.

When her stare skipped over his face and down his body, his cock gave a hard twitch, coming alive at the obvious lust on her beautiful features. The ripe pink of her lips drew him in, lassoed his heart. Damn, he was hog-tied by this woman and she didn't even freakin' know how much she owned him.

Reaching out, she offered her hand to him. He took it, enclosing the soft, delicate one in his own hardened one. His hands had killed while hers only healed. They came from such opposite worlds—could it even work if they tried?

"Come with me." She tugged on his hand, and he followed, unable to find some control to deny her. Walking away at this point was probably best, but damn if he could summon the will.

He'd seen her room before, last time he was here. All the windows were secure but if he had his way, he'd place a firearm in her nightstand drawer for protection. The space, however, was tidy and feminine, just like her. Shades of white on walls and bedding with a few touches of rose and some white marble accents with gray veining completed the space.

She let go of his hand and stood before him. "That was one exciting afternoon."

He cocked a brow. "Exciting?" She had been scared to the point of paleness that had worried him. Maybe it was his turn to take on the therapist role and force her to tell him her feelings.

When he reached for her, she moved her hands to her waist instead. He watched as she pulled her blouse out of her skirt and then began unbuttoning it. Bit by bit, her creamy flesh was revealed and his cock grew harder and harder.

Need pulsed in his veins. Battle wood, it was called, when a man got aroused following an adrenaline rush. This time it had everything to do with Atalee being within touching distance of him and the memory of her soft ass in his lap before the gunman had shown up.

He groaned as she dropped her top, revealing a lacy white bra with see-through bits. He wet his lips but didn't move a muscle, too mesmerized with the striptease.

Her breasts strained forward as she reached behind her back and unclasped her bra. It loosened around her ribs and dipped to show off two perfect mounds, the centers set with rosy hard nipples.

Cock fully distended now, he nudged himself into a more comfortable position behind his fly but it did no good. When he was this hard, fitting in his jeans didn't always work out well. Even now, the tip was nudging up over the waist of his boxers.

Her blonde hair tumbled around her shoulders, caressing her nipples as she reached for her skirt. A hidden zipper slid down, and she stepped out of the fabric.

In only tiny baby blue panties, she was the stuff of a Victoria Secret's catalog, but to him she was so much more.

He knew what sort of mind lived behind the pretty face and the sweetness of her heart. His throat closed as he took a step forward.

"Shaw..."

"I'm so damn sorry about what happened, baby doll."

She cupped his jaw, running the pad of her thumb back and forth over the scruff growing there. "You shouldn't be apologizing—I should be thanking you."

His chest expanded and he held his breath. "I'm not the man you knew." His voice hitched.

"No. We're both different." She threaded their fingers, eyes so earnest as she stared up at him as if he was the only man in the world. He didn't deserve that. When she tugged him by the hand toward the bed, he was helpless to do anything but follow.

She shoved him down and wedged her naked body between his splayed knees. "Let's find out who we are now."

When she kissed him, his heart exploded with love and his balls grew heavy with need. He put his hands on her—who wouldn't?—and let them glide over her slippery nakedness. She crawled onto his lap, straddling him, and the fresh scent of her arousal struck his senses.

With a growl, he deepened the kiss while rolling her onto the mattress, exploring every inch of her with his hands.

"Taste me, Shaw." She cupped one breast, and the rosy tip begged for his tongue.

Lowering his head with a groan, he captured her nipple and felt his world shift into a peaceful state where only happiness and pleasure lived.

* * * * *

Each nibble and lick Shaw placed around her nipples sent more and more need squeezing through her body. Her insides clutched, and she sank her fingertips into his shoulders, drawing him closer.

He released a groan that rumbled through her system in the sexiest of ways. When he looked up into her eyes and purposely ran his tongue around her areola, her breath caught in her lungs. She couldn't look away from this gorgeous, tough guy who lived on the edge and made her feel completely safe.

As he trailed his angled jaw down between her breasts, she let out a shuddering breath of anticipation. He traveled over her ribs, abdomen and paused with his mouth hovering over her mound as he rested between her legs.

His skin was warm steel beneath her fingers as she guided him right where she wanted him. A second before he parted his lips over her pussy, his eyes flashed like a bolt of blue lightning.

Liquid heat passed from his mouth to her pussy, and he immediately gave a sucking pull on her clit. Driving her up fast and hard.

She bucked forward, and he drove a finger inside her sheath.

After that, she was only aware of sensations passing through her, barely discernable as movements but only feelings as he pleasured her toward a pinnacle she'd never reached before.

Her inner thighs quaked around his ears. He twisted his tongue around her clit and then down her wet seam to dip into her pussy alongside his finger. When she moaned, he thrust another finger inside her, high, hard, plunging now with both as he worked his tongue frantically over her nubbin.

A release shook her with a loud cry. Waves pounded her. Bliss stole her mind, and until Shaw was poised to enter her, she floated on ecstasy.

His lips and jaw were wet with her juices, and he didn't wipe them away as he sank balls-deep between her thighs.

Wrapping her arms around him, she dragged him down for a kiss, sharing her flavors and enticing a growl from him. With her ankles tucked behind the hard planes of his ass, she held him in place, deep.

"I feel you throbbing," she rasped.

The corner of his lips twitched. "You're gonna feel my hot cum in a second." He jerked upward, breaking her ankles' hold on him, and fucked her in one smooth glide. Then another and another until they were galloping toward an end that was already rocking her world.

Passion rose up to twine around the blissful sensations. She buried her face against his neck and snaked her tongue over his salty skin.

"You feel so damn perfect," he bit off, hips churning faster, disjointedly.

Suddenly, he changed rhythm, slowing his pace and dragging his thickness through her wet walls. A low cry left her, and her pussy pulsated. The abrupt shift had her on the ledge of orgasm again.

How did he drive her to it so quickly? The man only had to look into her eyes to send her pulse racing and make her panties soaked. But being in bed with him...

She never wanted him to leave it.

"Kiss me as I come," she said in a rush.

Another growl twisted his lips as he claimed her mouth, sinking his tongue in time to his cock. When the peak of pleasure hit, she was so wrapped up in him that she knew the split second that he let go for her as well.

* * * * *

Atalee woke with confusion tearing at her. She stared at her dark surroundings, but everything was as usual—her bedroom was the same quiet, peaceful space it always was.

Then she caught the trace of Shaw's scent and realized what was wrong.

He wasn't in bed.

She sat up and swung her legs over the mattress. She was completely naked, so she grabbed the first thing she saw, which was his shirt, and put it on. He wouldn't have left without his shirt, so that must mean he was around here someplace.

"Shaw?" Her voice was dulled by the silence with only the hum of the refrigerator in the other room answering.

Moving through her house, she didn't find him in the bathroom or living room. Following the whir of the fridge, she walked into the kitchen thinking he might be getting a drink. The back door stood open.

Slipping outside, she welcomed the rush of cooler night air on her bare legs. Her deck was the size of a postage stamp, with only room for a couple chairs and tiny table that held a drink or two. And Shaw was seated in one of the chairs, elbows resting on his knees and his face in his hands.

Panic swept her, waking her fully. She moved to him and when she touched his bare shoulder, he came alive, sitting back in his chair and reaching for her.

She slid into his arms, and he drew her across his lap with her legs over his hard thighs. He wore only boxers, and the hair on his legs tickled against her skin.

"Are you okay?" she asked, though it was clear from the tension coiled in his muscles that he wasn't.

"Bad dreams." His voice was pitched low but overflowed with torment.

Her heart reached out to him, and she leaned into his chest. "Talk to me. Whatever comes out, I'll listen. Just please talk to me."

He started in Mexico, words falling from his lips in broken fragments until she gathered that he'd taken the life of a young man who'd been about to shoot Shaw. And how ever since, Shaw saw the boy's face on others during missions.

When he came to a finish, he seemed wrung out, slumping in the chair.

"Now that I know what you're battling, I can try to help you," she said.

He nodded, moving his hand up to settle on her nape, holding her to his chest. "I don't know why it even plagues me — I know plenty of police or Texas Rangers who've done what was necessary in the line of duty and don't think twice on it. But this has made me second-guess my actions more than once, and it can't continue if I'm going to stay with Ranger Ops."

"Do you want to stay in the special forces?"

He nodded at once. "It's where I belong, where I do most good in this world."

She wasn't about to make this about herself and tell him that it frightened her, being in love with a man who faced such danger on a daily basis. Fact was, she could lose him at any moment, and she'd be left to carry on without him.

"Then we have to get things straight in your mind, help you grieve for that boy."

"Grieve?" The word came out as a gulp of surprise.

She nodded. "I think in this case, what you're feeling isn't unlike what those who've been in a car accident with a loved one and lost that person have experienced. Some survivor's guilt, some guilt that they lost their life at your hands."

He swallowed hard. Under her ear, his heart thumped away without a hitch to give away what he thought about what she'd said.

After a minute, she tipped her head to look up at him. In the low light, his eyes glittered black.

"You're good for me." His voice was rough as he drew her head back down to his chest.

"I'm here as long as you need me, Shaw. We'll do it together, okay?"

His only response was a flex of his arms around her body, enfolding her tight. They sat there a long time looking at the moon before heading back to bed.

Once she was cuddled against his side, he ran a hand over her backside. "I want you bad, but is it okay to just lie here and be quiet?"

Love sprang up in her heart and overflowed through the rest of her body. She latched a hand onto his shoulder and curled closer. "Of course, Shaw. I just love being next to you."

When she woke, he wasn't in bed and only a scribbled note told her that she wouldn't see him for a while — he'd been called out on a mission.

Chapter Eight

"Man, I left a naked woman in my bed for this?" Linc's drawl had half the Ranger Ops team shaking with laughter. He turned his head to look at Shaw next to him, kitted out in full gear of cammies, helmet, half a dozen gadgets and weapons strapped to his person and his night vision scope to his eye as he evaluated the situation and attempted to stop thinking about the woman he'd left in bed too. Hell, he hadn't even taken the opportunity to make her scream in pleasure one last time, and he may never return to her.

Linc let out a snort and directed his attention on the woods between them and the sonsabitches that officials were saying had enough firepower for a real fight. Knight Ops had arrived by Chinook chopper, and they were spread out across a line of force to be reckoned with. They had enough firepower of their own.

"I'm tellin' ya," Linc went on. "Long legs."

"Tanned?" Lennon asked at his side.

"Freckled."

"Oh Jesus. It's a wonder you climbed out from between them then. You always did have a thing for fair women." Lennon raised his binoculars. "Fuckin' A, I caught a flash just now."

"I saw it too," came one of the Knights through their comms. "Shit, it's HE, one mike out."

Highly explosives one minute out.

Nash had Cavanaugh moving in as breacher, the first to scope out the area, and the Knight brother who dealt most explosives angled through the trees to meet up with him. A minute later, Cav filled them in on what he'd found, and they would have stepped into, if they hadn't seen that flash of light on an electronic fuse.

"Well, that won't just blow our balls off. We'd be six feet under." Shaw's words were met with grunts of agreement.

Nash ordered Cav and Rhoades Knight to pick apart what they could of the wiring and hurry back. "Woody, you're with me," Nash said.

Shaw unfolded from his position on one knee, weapon raised against any threat he happened across. His mind hovered on the present, and for that he was grateful—he didn't have room in this mission for errors or ghosts.

As he and Nash converged, one of the Knights met up with them. "I'm Ben," he said, low.

"Woody."

132

Nash shot Ben a grin, teeth white in the face paint he wore. "Nash."

"I know your ass. Could smell ya from ten paces." Ben's words had others chuckling in their ears, and Nash went out ahead a step or two, head and weapon swaying in sync as he attempted to root out the bastards looking to ambush them.

A second later, Nash held up a hand for them to stop. Ben edged up to Shaw. "Keep your balls tucked."

Shaw nodded.

The ground under his boots felt crunchy with sticks and leaves, and he shifted ever so slightly to keep anything from cracking and giving away their positions.

"Shaw Woodward?" Ben asked.

"Yeah."

"Heard what happened to ya in Mexico with that kid." Ben's statement had Shaw's gut clenching. That was the last thing he wanted to hear right now. His first instinct was to call Ben an asshole for bringing it up, but he bit back his words out of respect.

"It's tough shit to deal with," Ben went on.

Why the hell was he dredging this shit up? Shaw felt his fingers begin to ache from gripping his rifle so tight.

A heartbeat passed where Shaw waged an internal war on any residual effects of that fucking mission, beating them back where he could function.

"Had somethin' similar in Afghanistan," Ben said.

Now Shaw was listening. "What did you do to get rid of it?" He was aware that every Knight Ops and Ranger Ops man could hear their conversation and didn't even care, if it meant he received some helpful advice — and they might too.

"Lock it in a mental box." Ben never glanced Shaw's way, involved in watching their position. Shaw's gaze was riveted on the forest too, estimating how far they stood from the front line of enemies on the border. The bastards wouldn't have a beef with them for long, because they'd all be dust.

Shaw thought on his words, and Ben continued. "Shit like that can't be dwelled on, because fact is, I'd do it again if I had to."

Nash gave the signal for them to move on, and Shaw crept around trees, careful of roots. He couldn't help but think this was a bit like hunting deer or hogs in Texas.

Thinking on Ben's words, Shaw didn't know if he could say he'd do it again. Maybe that kid didn't have to be taken out along with the others — he could have been spared. The flip side was that the teen would have shot him, or if Shaw had stopped him first, the boy would have grown up to be a criminal anyway. There was no rehab for people like him. Often, it was gang-related or a family business.

Shaw shoved the thoughts down, thankful when his hard-ass take-no-prisoners mentality shifted into place right when he needed it.

Nash got the others on their feet and moved up swiftly next to them. The first bright flash of light preceded the blast of sound as an explosion went off a short distance from Shaw's right. He and Nash dived out of range, but the repercussion knocked his feet out from under him, and he pitched up next to a tree.

Shaw began to right himself, digging his knees into the ground and pushing upward even as he evaluated his own body for injuries.

A hand got under him, and he scrambled upward. "Okay, man?" Ben asked.

"I'm good."

Then Nash gave the word, and they were in the fight of their lives, rushing down a dirt hill between trees in a line, the green glow of their night vision lighting their way. The first shots came from the Knight Ops.

Shaw fired on movement beyond some underbrush. "Don't let those Louisiana boys show us up now!"

"Guts and glory!" someone called out, and since it was a motto to all, morale spiked. They opened fire.

For ten solid minutes, it rained bullets. One sheared off a branch over Jess's head, and he was knocked to the ground. Lennon checked him out before they rejoined the fray. Shaw's mind was laser-focused on keeping his life and those of the men around him.

Maybe he'd exorcised his ghosts once and for all. Whether it was Atalee's doing or Ben's advice, there wasn't a damn one in sight.

An arm came around his neck. His feet went out from under him a second time, and he kicked even as he jammed the heel of his hand into the nose of the man holding him. He didn't release Shaw, only dragged him backward. Jerking his rifle around, he jammed it into the man's side and pulled the trigger.

Air flowed back into his lungs as the man crumpled in a pool of blood. Shaw looked up in time to see Linc's body vanish over a rise.

A battle cry sounded, and it took Shaw a moment to realize it was coming from him. His body shook with rage. He waved to Ben, and together they launched after Linc.

He wasn't fucking there.

Not even a body on the ground.

"They captured him," Shaw bit off. Fury welled in massive waves inside him, cresting and breaking. He and Ben zigzagged around the area, following tracks in the dark, but it was damn near impossible when the bastards had walked all over the ground here.

Nash took up the search along with another Knight, scouring all the underbrush for a body.

Linc wasn't fucking here.

136

"Spread out. Linc's off the map. Linc, can you hear us?" Nash's voice held a roughened edge that wasn't exactly the calm Shaw and the Ranger Ops team were used to from their captain.

The hair on Shaw's neck prickled and he swung to the right just as a man jumped up. Shaw sprayed him with bullets. Men leaped out from behind trees and crawled over the rise like ants at a picnic. Even after Ranger Ops and Knight Ops had taken out that terrorist platoon, a second wave hit the forest.

Shaw whipped right and left, picking people off as fast as they came at them. He had to fucking end this, because he was going to find Linc.

* * * * *

Atalee walked her patient to the door. "Have a good week, Rob. Try to use some of the coping mechanisms we talked about."

"I will. See you next week, Dr. Franklin." He nodded in farewell and disappeared down the hall.

She watched him go for a moment, but her mind was already moving away from the session and on to other matters.

Like the fact that it had been nine days since she'd heard from Shaw. How did military wives do this on a daily basis? As a Doctor of Psychology, she was cool and collected enough to realize her imagination was getting ahead of her. But as a woman who cared about Shaw, the worry and stress were eating her up.

In some ironic twist she was looking at her own emotions from a therapist's point of view, analyzing her reactions to things and thinking of way she could cope better just like she'd told Rob half an hour ago.

Here she was on the other end of the rope, and she didn't feel strong enough to win this tug of war.

Maybe it was best to forget about a relationship with Shaw. Sure, she'd imagined how it would be, but that was before she realized he was in much deeper than she'd believed. It was time to do some research on what spouses of military men and women did to pass the time when they had no idea when they'd next see their loved one.

Atalee lifted a hand to her brow and massaged her forehead. The light ache behind it was stress, she knew.

The other issue plaguing her was whether or not she and Shaw were really a thing. They'd only had a few stolen moments in life together. But at one time, he had believed professing his love so important that he'd been driven to say it before she walked down the aisle. She could only guess that his feelings hadn't changed since.

After a minute, she went out to the receptionist's desk. Danielle looked up with a smile. "What can I do for you, Dr. Franklin?"

"Has there been any word from Sh—" she quickly corrected herself " —from Joe Beck?"

She leafed through some pages and then looked up at Atalee. "I'm afraid not."

Atalee chewed on her lip.

"I've seen it before. These are tough guys, and they believe getting mental help makes them lesser men. They are often pushed to seek help, but after a session or two vanish."

Atalee felt herself nodding. Of course, she knew all this. But she had so much more invested in Shaw.

"Thank you." She turned for her office again. She fiddled with some paperwork littering her desk while waiting for her last patient of the day, who finally cancelled.

You can't help them all.

With a heavy sigh, she pushed away from her desk. The only thing to do was find some ease for herself in hope that her scattered thoughts started to make sense. She'd start with a run, catch up on laundry, maybe stop in to see how her momma was doing on that room. She had a sneaking suspicion that her mother was ignoring it and no progress had been made without Atalee cracking the whip.

On her way out, the head of the department, Dr. Norman, stopped her, waving her into his office.

She pressed a smile onto her face. "How are you doing today, Doctor?"

"Fine, fine. Please have a seat. Wait, do you have a moment to talk? I should have asked you that first." The man had a pleasant face with thick white hair waving back from a face surprisingly unlined for a man in his mid-sixties.

She gave a small chuckle and took a chair across his desk. "Yes, I have time."

Dr. Norman sank to his desk chair and folded his hands over his middle as he contemplated her. "How do you find things here at the hospital?"

"I love it. The office is very pleasant and runs like a well-oiled machine."

He opened his mouth to speak, when a rap on the door had them both turning in their seats. Danielle walked in, and from the expression she wore, something was concerning her.

Atalee jumped up, and Dr. Norman followed.

"There's an emergency coming in."

"Why weren't we buzzed?" Dr. Norman asked.

"The man hasn't hit the ER yet." She sliced a look at Atalee. "A man named Nash Sullivan called ahead."

Atalee's stomach dropped to the toes of her pumps, and she gripped the chair arm to steady herself. If Nash was calling, the emergency must be Shaw. She pictured the worst, the man she loved in a comatose state after enduring some other trauma that had finally tipped him over the edge.

"I'm on my way down." Atalee rushed out the door, skirting Danielle. She hit the elevator before Dr. Norman even came into sight, so she went ahead and descended to the ground floor without him.

Her mind scrambled over the mountains she was about to help Shaw climb. If he was truly —

The doors opened, and she surged out, heading down a corridor that led directly to the ER. With each step that carried her closer, her heart pounded harder.

Shaw, I'm coming.

She only prayed she could help him. Or that he wasn't already lost to her.

* * * * *

"Call in the burn team and we need wound care. That gash on his leg has been festering for days from the looks of it." The triage doctor called out orders to everyone around them, and Shaw took it all in, but he was really waiting for one person.

He looked to Nash. "You called Atalee's office?"

Nash nodded, mouth set into a straight line.

A movement caught Shaw's eye, and he jerked his head to the side as a familiar blonde sailed into the room. She came to a dead stop, staring at the bandaged man on the bed. Her face pinched, and then she gave an all over shudder.

Shaw made an involuntary noise in his throat, and she twisted sharply. Her gaze latched onto his, and she hurled herself forward into his arms. He caught her up, mouth finding hers without even thinking of where they were and who would see.

She clung to him for a long heartbeat, trembling. Then suddenly, she pushed away and turned to the gurney where Linc lay, drifting in and out of consciousness. In the wee hours, Shaw had discovered him half buried in the silt of a river. His heart had nearly given out at the sight, but following days of relentless searching, they'd finally found their teammate.

After turning Linc over, he'd shouted that he was still breathing, and they'd evacuated him and assessed his injuries while in flight. The burns from explosives to his legs were most worrisome, and that gash *was* festering, as the triage doctor had said. But the scariest thing, in Shaw's opinion, was the way Linc seemed to stare through them, as if he wasn't seeing the men who fought next to him and had spent sleepless nights searching for him. As if Linc was really seeing ghosts of his own.

A nurse poked her head in. "I've got a Colonel Downs on the phone, demanding that this man is stabilized and moved immediately to Washington DC."

Nash stood. "Do as he instructs, then." He looked to Shaw. "You got this, First Lieutenant?"

Shaw nodded.

"I'm going home to Nevaeh."

Shaw stood and clapped him on the back in a hard embrace only men who'd seen true horror together could share. "I'll stay by him till he's transported."

Atalee was watching their exchange. When Nash left, she pulled Shaw aside. Her touch on his arm shocked him. Following days of pain, despair and balls-out battle, he'd almost forgotten how gentleness could affect him.

"I'm not sure they can do much for your friend at this point." She searched his eyes. "The most the critical care doctor can do is order something to calm him, but the painkillers he's given will do that and they're more crucial right now."

Shaw gave a jerky nod, emotion cutting through him. "I can't begin to guess what they did to him."

"Was he captured?" She pitched her voice low.

He nodded. Unable to say more, he moved up to the bed and looked down at his friend. Linc's breathing was labored. As he looked on, a nurse administered a drug into the IV they'd started the minute he hit the hospital doors.

Shaw gripped Linc's hand. "I'm here for ya, brother. They'll take good care of you here and then you'll be shipped to DC."

Linc only stared at him, giving Shaw no sign that he understood what he was saying.

"You're gonna be all right, man. We're all here for you." His throat threatened to close up, and he felt Atalee's hand on his spine, offering him the support he needed.

"We're going to have to ask you to leave. We're moving him to the burn unit to asses the damage to his legs." The nurse looked to Shaw.

He nodded. "Don't ship him out until I've said goodbye, you hear?"

At the hard command in his voice, she answered with a quick nod. Atalee took Shaw's arm and led him out of the room. She didn't take him into the public waiting room but to a space for employees only. When she closed the door and turned those big eyes of hers on him, he cracked.

Dipping his head, he dug his thumb and forefinger into each eye, stopping any emotion that would surface.

"Shaw." She put her arms around him, and he bowed his face into her fragrant hair, inhaling her shampoo and pure womanly smell. "Thank God you got that man back. He will be given top-of-the-line medical care and the best chances to heal. You gave him that chance by rescuing him."

He nodded. "I've been a whiny baby, dwelling on the shit I've done. Compared to what Linc dealt with, it seems like a summer vacation."

"Don't downplay what you've faced. But yes, many have their own crosses to bear. God, it's good to hold you in my arms." She tipped her face up, all sexy secretary in her glasses again, and he couldn't resist those tempting lips. They were one of the things that had kept him going, especially the past few days when circumstances really looked the fucking worst.

144

As he lowered his mouth to hers, it was like he could finally breathe again.

He broke the kiss. "Baby doll. God, you're beautiful." He cupped her jaw and drank in her features. "When all hell broke loose, the thought of getting back to you was the only thing that kept me going. I know years ago I told you that I loved you, and you weren't able to process it then. I hope now things are changed between us. Because Atalee, I love you so fucking much, and all I could think about on the way here was telling you, making you understand that you're my world and always have been."

Her lips parted on a sigh. "Oh Shaw..." Her throat worked, and her eyes brightened with tears. "You have no idea how long I've been thinking about this... How much I started to fall in love with you."

Jesus. He didn't deserve to hear those words—after all the shit he'd put her through, she should be shoving him away and telling him to leave.

She reached up to cradle his jaw with her hands, rubbing the soft pads of her thumbs over his full beard that had grown in over the past days. He was dirty and probably smelled—all he'd managed to do was brush his teeth and strip off some layers of gear down to his cammies, and he'd been wearing those for too long.

Dipping his mouth to hers, he kissed her long and thoroughly, until he felt her sag in his hold. After a long moment, he withdrew and searched her eyes. "I'm going to take you home and keep you in my bed till you can't walk. But right now..." The look they exchanged told him they both wanted that, but Linc came first.

She took him by the hand. "Let's go see if there's any new information on your friend. Then you can take me home."

"And shower."

She eyed him with a spark in her eyes. "But not shave."

Damn, she knew how to make a man's cock hard.

Chapter Nine

While Shaw saw Linc off, she gave him the space he needed to say things he might not wish to say in front of her. She waited patiently in the quiet employee room, thinking on everything that had happened.

A man came into the room and fed dollar bills into the vending machine. He gave her a smile and short greeting, which she returned. Then he took his drink and potato chips and left.

The minutes trundled by slowly, and she was beginning to wonder if something had happened with Linc, when he poked his head into the room. She stood at once and went to his side.

"He's being air-lifted right now."

She'd heard the chopper on the roof and wondered if the medi-vac was for Linc.

Sliding her arms around Shaw, she said, "He's in good hands."

He squeezed her for a moment before letting her go. Then he took her hand and led her out.

Something was different about Shaw. Despite the stress he must be under after what happened to his friend, Linc, he seemed strangely... at peace.

Atalee stole glance after glance at his profile as they navigated the hospital corridors to the exit. "Did you drive?"

"I came with Nash and Linc."

She couldn't imagine the worry he and Nash must have been under all the way to the hospital. Linc was in bad shape.

Reaching over, she caught Shaw's hand in her own. "At least he's stable and will get top-notch care in DC."

"He fucking better." His lips were set in a firm, no-bullshit line, and a shiver trickled through her, like someone squeezing a wet sponge over her head. What she knew of Shaw when he was friends with her ex—that he was capable of taking care of whatever business was thrown his way—was amplified since he'd gone from Texas Ranger to Ranger Ops.

She wouldn't ever want to be on this man's bad side—she'd seen firsthand what he was capable of with the guy at the park. The expression Shaw wore told her without a doubt that if Linc didn't receive what he needed as far as care went, Shaw would be paying somebody a visit.

In the dark of night.

She tightened her hold on his hand as she led him to where her car was parked in the doctors' lot. When they reached her vehicle, he turned to her. "Mind if I drive?"

She shook her head. If driving gave him what he needed — control, distraction — she was all for it. She rummaged in her handbag for her keychain.

When he closed his fingers around it, he stared into her eyes. "You should always have your keys out and at the ready so you're not standing in plain view and giving somebody more chance to attack you."

She blinked. "I think we're relatively safe here in the lot. Even at night, there's plenty of lighting."

He gave a noncommittal grunt and opened her door for her first. She slid in, and then he climbed behind the wheel. Drawing her hand to his lips, he brushed a kiss over her knuckles that seared a scorching-hot path to her belly… and lower.

"Everything is going to be okay this time," he said.

Her stomach pitched at his words. "I made a bad choice in men the last time, and I have no intention of making it twice."

What could only pass as a smile ghosted over his rugged features. Then he released her hand and put the car in drive.

When a siren sounded, he swung his head toward it, but they were too far away from the source.

"You know you can talk to me, right?" she asked.

149

"Already been debriefed." He gave her another smile.

"Okay... While I love seeing that smile on your face, I can't help but be a little worried about you. Are you sure you're all right?"

"I'm on American soil, there's an American flag flying on practically every city block and we all got home with our lives. I'm about to stand under the hot water for half an hour and then I'm going down on my girl and lick her pussy till she's soaking."

Her insides clutched at his words, and her nipples drew up tight.

His blue eyes burned her way. "And while she's still coming, I'm going to push my hard cock into her and fuck her" —he drew out the words— "till she's hoarse from screaming."

After a pounding heartbeat, she found her voice. "Then what?" She sounded out of breath.

"A pizza."

She tossed her head back and laughed. Damn, it felt good too. She was happy to see the man she loved less conflicted—dare she say carefree?

No, she wouldn't go that far. He still bore creases between his brows that seemed etched there since the last time they'd been together. She couldn't even guess at what extreme measures he'd taken to get Linc back.

In time, she hoped he grew to trust her enough to tell her these things if it granted him ease.

"Tell me what you've been doing since I saw you." He sliced a heavy-lidded glance her direction.

She tucked her knees together to quell the need he raised in her. "I've sort of forced a project on my mother."

"What sort of project?"

"She had a hoarder room."

He grunted a laugh. "A hoarder room?"

"Yes. I didn't realize how awful it was, because I never have a reason to go into that space. So we've been slowly sorting, purging and organizing. Just when I think we're getting to the finish line, we unearth more boxes of junk, though now I think we're almost finished. She was supposed to do a few more things this week, but I have a feeling she's been off playing tennis with her girlfriends at the club."

"Can't blame her."

"It's no fun, that's true. But it has given me something to do."

He squeezed her hand. "I'm sorry, Atalee. I know you've been worrying."

She nodded. "Now I'm looking forward to..." she ran her finger suggestively over his palm, "pizza."

"I'm ready to eat." He arched a brow, turning her inside out with want. They couldn't reach his house fast enough and when they got out, she hurried to keep up with his long legs. She proved too slow for him, and he grabbed her into his arms, making her squeal, and carried her through the door.

He crushed his mouth over hers, steering her through the house, managing not to bump into any furniture and peeling off her workwear at the same time.

Inside his bathroom, he stopped, and with hands on her upper arms, said, "Step out of those panties."

The order sent slick need between her legs, and she quivered as she hooked her thumbs in her panties and let them fall.

His gaze, hot and hungry, washed over her. Bare naked, she stepped up to him and took hold of his shirt hem. He watched her intensely as she stripped it over his head and then went for his belt buckle, not the one that bore his name as she was used to, but a simple military issue. The front of his cargo pants swelled outward to meet her touch as she lowered his zipper.

As soon as her fingers moved over his erection, he let out a groan. She branded him with her touch, following the coiled length in his boxers to the tip and then freeing it from his underwear.

"Step out of those pants and boxers," she ordered.

A smile tipped the corner of his mouth but vanished as soon as it appeared when he bent to untie his boots and kicked the entire mass of clothing to the corner of the bathroom.

"I hate to tell you to take off your glasses — they're so damn sexy."

Pleasure ran over her as she slipped the frames off her face and set them safely on the counter.

"Turn on the shower." His command rolled off his lips, rolling over her as well. Nipples puckered, she turned her back to him and made a show of leaning over to switch on the water, jutting her backside his direction.

"Damn, I'm gonna claim that ass of yours one of these days. I know you've never been touched there."

She went still, heart beating loudly over the rush of water flowing into the shower. Johnny hadn't been all that into sex after marriage and he surely wouldn't have asked for anal sex.

The idea of it with Shaw, though... Her breaths came faster.

When he planted his callused hands on her waist, spreading his fingers down over her belly and then lower, sinking his fingers into the curls on her mound, she leaned back against his hard chest with a sigh of pleasure.

His hard cock pressed against her ass, and he growled low in his throat. "You don't know what fighting does to a man. I've been hard a dozen times since walking away from you, and there's so much cum built up in my balls that I'm going to keep my dick in you a long time."

Each word rumbled past her ear sent new fire to her pussy, and she wiggled against him. He lashed an arm around her waist and drew her back as he eased one hand down to cup her pussy.

Juices squeezed from her. He ran a finger down her seam to her drenched hole and back up to her clit, taking his time to drive her crazy. Breathing fast, she widened her stance to give him total access. When he dipped a fingertip into her pussy, she flooded again.

Suddenly, he lifted her over the lip of the shower and under the spray. Water poured over her hair and down her shoulders, the warmth zigzagging over her curves. Shaw stepped in behind her, flattening her to the wall. With his big body trapping her and his hard lips hovering over hers, she was close to coming.

She looped her hand around his nape and pulled him down.

* * * * *

Shaw's mind skipped over and over—*soaked, she needs me, taste her*. He let himself go and allowed only sensations and emotions to take over. On duty, he was a machine, following orders and sticking to protocol. But here, alone with Atalee, they were free.

He planted himself between her thighs and reached to the ledge for the soap. The pump dispenser came in handy, and he prided himself on that decision on his last shopping trip.

With a palm full of soap, he looked into her eyes before very pointedly rubbing his soapy hands together. She trembled and bit into her lower lip, tugging at the flesh in a way that told him she was on edge.

Fuck, it turned him on. He'd keep her riding that ledge as long as possible before he let her come.

Starting at her shoulders, he ran his hands in small circles down her chest to her breasts, circling each nipple until it puckered into a hardness he ached to feel on his tongue. Then lower — to her stomach, splaying over her hips and finally he dipped one hand between her legs.

He soaped her pussy with slow movements that were driving her wild. She arched upward, and he latched his mouth onto her neck, nibbling up and down as he eased one finger and then two into her tight heat.

She clamped around his invasion, almost sucking him in. He plunged his fingers higher, feeling her drench him with juices again. "Give me your mouth," he grated out.

She tipped her head up, and their lips collided in a long, tongue-tangling kiss as he plunged his fingers into her again and again and again. She rose onto tiptoes, emitting tiny moans into his mouth. He hardened another fraction.

He slipped his thumb over her clit, depressing it lightly. She cried out and curled forward as her first orgasm hit.

But there were many more to be had.

He drew it out with soft flicks of his thumb and finished by pumping his fingers in a slow rhythm as she came down from her high. As she slumped against the wall, he gave her a crooked smile and reached for the soap again.

This time he scrubbed himself from head to toes, washing all the grime of days in the field down the drain. With his cock jutting out, he reached for her once more.

As he lifted her against him, she wrapped her arms and legs around him. His cock head rubbed at her slick folds, and she rocked downward, taking him inside her in one quick glide.

His balls throbbed, tucked tight against her body, and he planted a hand on her ass to hold her in place as he began to move.

He needed all the control he could get.

"Shaw," she breathed against his lips. Love shone in her eyes.

"I'm never giving you up again."

"I love you."

Her words hit him. His heart swelled and his cock lengthened as the first jet of cum shot up. He gripped her tight and pumped out another. She tightened around him with her own orgasm, and her throaty cry echoed off the shower walls.

His release went on for what felt like minutes, with his mind floating in euphoria and his woman in his arms. He dipped his tongue between her lips, and she kissed him back as they came down together.

Suddenly, all his sleepless nights caught up to him, and he sagged. He lifted her off his cock with another kiss promising more as soon as he recovered and let her slide down to her feet.

She dug her fingers into his shoulders, kneading at his sore muscles. He issued a groan and let his forehead drop to the wall over her head.

"Let's get out," she said.

"You sapped the last of my energy."

"I plan to sap a lot more, so grab those towels and take me to bed."

They managed to towel off and make it to his bed which, thanks to his cleaning lady, had clean sheets. When he collapsed onto the mattress, his eyes instantly shut.

Then he felt it.

Atalee's hot mouth moving over his thighs.

When she reached his balls, gently mouthing him, he tangled his fingers into her hair and guided her lips up and over his hard cock.

* * * * *

She knew what love wasn't—she'd lived that once before. And looking at Shaw propped against the sofa with his long legs stretched in front of him eating pizza, she knew what it was.

After her failed marriage, she imagined herself living a single life, working, finding exciting hobbies to busy herself—and taking a lover now and then to break up the monotony.

Never did she believe she would find something that felt like this... so right.

As Shaw brought his slice of extra-meat topping pizza to his lips, she watched him. God, he was even hot as hell when he ate. That chiseled jaw moved in all the ways that would drive a woman insane with want.

She tucked her legs up as she reached for a second slice.

"You need to catch up. I'm on my fourth."

"I didn't just slay dragons and you did."

He cocked his head. "You do every day, baby doll. Don't you realize how much you help people?"

Pride rose up, but she also let out a giggle. "You never sat on my couch long enough to talk through anything and know how much I can help."

"We don't need a couch. We take care of it in bed."

Warmth slithered through her, and she smiled before taking a bite. The garlic and tomato flavors mixed on her tongue, and she enjoyed each bite. She enjoyed the view of her man more.

"I want to take you out," he said out of the blue.

She straightened. "Okay."

"What do you say about heading to the ranch with me?"

"I'd love that. I haven't done anything outdoors except run in a while."

"My dad's still got a few horses. We could ride out to the creek. Pretty deep in some places, and in one, a natural dam makes a pool big enough for swimmin'." He wagged his brows. "Maybe skinny-dippin'."

She grinned, but her smile eased into an expression of concern when he gave a wide yawn that seemed to encompass his entire body, right down to his curling bare toes.

"You're still exhausted."

"Yeah, it was worse than hell week as a Navy Seal, from what I hear of the Seals. No sleep, full out tests at every turn."

Reaching over, she placed a hand on his. "But you came out on top."

"We weren't leaving till we got Linc back." He yawned again.

"Why don't you hit the sack and I'll put the pizza away."

"Do you promise to come lie next to me for a bit?"

Love bloomed in her core. "I'll be right in."

After she watched him get off the floor with surprising grace for a man of his size, she closed the lid of the pizza box and padded to the kitchen on bare feet wearing only his T-shirt. She put the box into the fridge and placed their glasses in the sink. By the time she got to the bedroom, she stopped in the doorway, staring at the huge special ops man face down on the mattress, dead to the world.

A smile touched her lips even as his light snore touched her heart. It frightened her how much she loved Shaw. If something ever happened to him, if by chance he didn't come back one day...

She closed the door on those thoughts and tiptoed to the bed. As soon as she curled up against his side, he flipped over enough to anchor an arm over her. She wasn't exactly tired but being close to a sleeping man made her drowsy even as his scents worked under her skin and stirred her libido.

Her eyes wandered over the scar on his chest she could see a hint of. Shaw carried so much on his shoulders. As a therapist, she might bring up the option of resigning from Ranger Ops.

He'd have more calm on some levels, but she also knew he'd return to the Texas Rangers, which dealt with their share of crimes. Why couldn't she have fallen in love with an accountant? Somebody who came home in the evening and kissed her at the door... played baseball in the back yard with their children.

Under her hand, his skin was warm steel. And she knew if she shook him awake, he had to ability to be wide-eyed and alert in a blink, because he was trained to. She followed the line of his shoulder down his arm, over the bulge of biceps and the cords and veins snaking to his wrist. So powerful, so tender. The juxtaposition had her thighs flexing together to stave off her need.

He needed his sleep.

But she needed him, to turn to her and touch her and make her feel loved before he went off again on another mission.

He gave a heavy stutter of breath, and in the end, she couldn't bring herself to wake him from the sleep he so badly needed. She cuddled him close.

* * * * *

When daylight broke through Shaw's eyelids, he woke instantly. Leaning up on his elbows, he looked around. His bed, his room, his house.

No danger.

No Atalee. Where was she?

Hell. It all rushed back. He'd promised her a date and then passed out for hours on her. Not the kind of impression he wanted to leave with her regarding their relationship. If he was going to keep her—and he goddamn well was—then he needed to step it up.

Jumping out of bed, he reached for some clothes—jeans, T-shirt and socks. After brushing his teeth, he grabbed his cowboy boots and hat on the way out of his room. "Baby doll?" he called out. "Atalee?"

He found her sitting on the couch swiping through images on her phone. She looked up with a smile and he was relieved to see no darkness in the depths of her beautiful eyes. He leaned in and kissed her. She moved into the caress, raising a moan from him.

"What are you doing?" he asked when he broke the kiss.

"Looking at things to help my mom finish organizing this room of hers. We planned to finish it over the weekend. If we don't display everything in a way she can see what she has, she'll only go buy like twenty more mascaras and stuff them in some box where she'll never find them again."

He sank down next to her. "What do you say we eat some cold pizza for breakfast and then get to the ranch?"

She giggled. "You just want to get to the skinny-dippin' part, don't you?"

He waggled his brows, urging another laugh from her. The sound was just as good as her cries of pleasure. "You've always been able to read me."

Her gaze ticked over his face, as if trying to determine if he was serious or not. He was.

"Don't you remember?" he asked.

"Remember what?"

"That day Johnny and I came back from covering that shootout down on Fifth? You kissed him, but you looked right at me and said, 'What happened?'"

She nodded slowly. "I do remember now. You had to make some hard choices that day, and I could see it wore on you."

"Yes." It was never easy. "Maybe I've always been left wondering if I made the right decision."

"You do," she said at once.

Drawing her hand into his, he looked into her eyes. "How do you know?"

"You're a good man, and you're level-headed, not rash. You only act when necessary. But Shaw—"

She broke off, just staring at him.

"What is it?"

"Have you ever thought about the toll this profession takes on you?"

Sure he had—plenty. But what was she getting at?

She directed her gaze to her lap. "I just wondered if..."

"Just say it." Damn, that came out harsher than he wanted. He softened his tone. "Please."

She met his gaze. "As a therapist, I would be remiss in my training if I didn't recommend that you continue to consider how your work affects you and explore the consequences of staying... or leaving it behind. What I hope for you as a former patient—or as someone I care more about more than a patient—is that you find peace of mind."

His mind blanked. "I have no idea what I'd do if I left Ranger Ops. What else is there for me? Would I take over the family ranch that already couldn't make a go of it?"

"I don't know. Just something that makes you happy."

He heard the worry in her voice and knew, deep down she was concerned about the dangers he faced though she would never say so. The notion warmed him, but he needed her to understand what kind of man he was. If they were going to be together, she had to know up front so she didn't make the same mistake as she had with Johnny.

After a long minute of silence, Shaw couldn't find a way to say what he felt. He cleared his throat and squeezed her hand. "Let's head out to the ranch for that date."

"It's barely eight in the morning."

"We'll get an early start. Maybe grill some steaks for lunch."

"That sounds good. I'll call my mom and let her know that she's off the hook on finishing that room today."

"You had plans? Don't break them."

She waved a hand. "Nothing set in stone. I only mentioned I might drop by. Believe me, she'd rather be going to one of her art exhibits or taking in a matinee than finish that room. Actually, I think she'd rather face a firing squad than finish it." She giggled.

"What if we invited her along?"

Her eyes widened. "To the ranch?"

"Yeah. My father could keep her company, show her around. He's got a good bottle of brandy he's been dying to crack open, and what better reason than on a woman?"

She gave him a sidelong look. "Are you matchmaking, Shaw Woodward?"

"Not at all. Just suggesting that they might enjoy each other's company while I enjoy yours." He couldn't hold back another minute and drew her across the sofa, plunking her into his lap. Her round bottom nestled over his groin, and his cock stirred.

Leaning in, he captured her lips. The kiss turned from heated to slow and thorough and back again before they pulled away.

He thumbed her lips. "God, I love kissin' you," he drawled.

The private smile he considered something she saved just for him—he'd never seen her give anybody else that smile—spread over her beautiful face. Easing his fingers under her thick hair, he gave her a crooked grin. "Let's get a move on."

After stopping off at her place for a change of clothes, they were on the road to his ranch and Atalee agreed to call her mother to invite her for lunch later.

"When was the last time you were here?" Atalee was fresh and bright in worn jeans, a plaid top knotted at the waist and boots for riding. She had her hair pulled into a ponytail and sunglasses perched on her head that made him think of those sexy glasses she drove him crazy with.

She clapped her hands, and he looked at her. Her mouth dropped open. "You weren't even listening to me, were you? What were you thinking about?"

"Peeling your skirt off you and taking you with your glasses on."

Her jaw dropped farther. "With my... Oh my." A flush coated her cheekbones, and she crossed her legs. But not before he slipped his hand between them and gave her pussy a seductive rub through her jeans.

Her head dropped against the seat. "You get me so worked up," she managed with a wavering voice.

"You do the same to me." He took his hand off the wheel long enough to adjust himself.

She gave him a teasing look and purposely ran her tongue over her lower lip, trapping him in a desire so strong that he nearly pulled over to ravish her. But somehow, he controlled himself long enough to reach the ranch.

Driving through the gates fed him a nostalgia so strong he almost tasted the biscuits and gravy his momma used to make before she'd passed on a while back.

"Fields need cut," he said as they rolled past the wood and iron gates bearing what used to be an upstanding brand in these parts. The W of Woodward

166

extended out on each side to curl into longhorns like the cattle they used to raise.

His mind went to Atalee's earlier comment about giving up special forces and finding something else to make him happy and find peace. If anything could, it would be this place.

As they navigated the gravel drive, he swung his head right and left, mentally noting improvements to be made—fence repairs, a tree that needed cut down after being struck by lightning.

Atalee was looking around with avid curiosity. "I've never been here. You have a sister, don't you? How is she?"

"Cammy. She's well, working as an ICU nurse out in Austin."

"That's fabulous. And your father—what does he do all day now without the cattle?"

"Mostly tinkers in his garage. He buys up old lawn mowers, ATVs and motorcycles and rebuilds them to sell. With land and house paid for, he doesn't need a whole lot to live on. Besides, he knows I'd help him any time he needs it."

"You're such a good son, Shaw." She touched his leg.

Sobering more than he already was, he stared at her. "I hope to be a good husband one day."

Speaking the words shouldn't feel as fine as whiskey slipping down his throat or sweet tea on a hot day, and damn if it wasn't even better. He savored the feel of them in his mouth and smiled at the woman he planned to make his wife.

He continued driving up to the house and parked the vehicle. They sat looking at the front of the home for a moment. Long and low with white siding and gray accents, another W on the front of the garage.

"A ways down, there's the barn." He pointed, and she followed his gesture.

He cut the engine and got out. As they converged in the yard and made their way to the front door, they clasped hands.

"What will your father think of this?" She swung their joined hands lightly.

He gazed down at her. "He's the one who urged me to tell you I loved you the day of your wedding."

Her lips parted on a gasp, and he continued up to the door. Without bothering to knock, he pushed it inward and called out, "Dad?"

"Shaw?" The voice came from what sounded like the depths of a closet.

"Yeah."

Keeping hold of Atalee's hand, he led her through the open front rooms to the kitchen. There was his father with his backside projecting from under the kitchen cabinet and plumbing tools scattered around him.

"Sprung a leak?" Shaw drawled.

One blue eye peered at him from the darkness of the cabinet as his father turned his head in the small space. "Hand me that fitting, would ya?"

Shaw grunted and let go of Atalee's hand to squat in front of the sink. He placed the fitting in his father's palm. His dad grunted in return. Behind him, Shaw heard a giggle from Atalee.

"Who ya got with ya, son?" came his father's muffled words along with some clinking of metal on metal.

"Atalee Franklin."

The noises from under the sink quieted. "That so?"

"Yeah." He twisted to look at Atalee. She had one arm folded over her middle and the other hand plastered to her mouth. Above her hand, her eyes twinkled with amusement.

After a second, the rattling came from within again as his father employed a wrench on a pipe and sealed the gap. Then he pushed out of the cabinet and onto his haunches. His hair was mussed, and he pushed it back as he settled his gaze on Atalee.

"Good to see ya, darlin'."

She dropped her hand and grinned. "You as well."

"I see my son finally got around to makin' things right."

Shaw stood and offered his dad a hand up. Feeling the old man's dry clasp in his own gave him

169

warm feelings of home and family. He brought his dad in for a hug, and Atalee let out a happy sigh.

The men turned to her with a chuckle. "Women," his father said with a shake of his head. "Always makin' us soft. Come and give me a hug too, darlin'." He walked toward Atalee with his arms extended, and they embraced. Seeing his girl in the arms of his family member made Shaw's throat close off.

Maybe I should marry her right now. As soon as we can get a license.

When his father stepped back, she gave them each a happy look. "Did you fix the sink, Mr. Woodward?"

"Now, I haven't seen you in a while, but you should know by now to call me Woody. Everyone and his uncle does in these parts. And yeah, I fixed it. I think. Give it a try, darlin." He waved toward the sink, and Atalee stepped up with much ceremony and turned on the faucet. All three of them peered under the sink for leaks, but there wasn't as much as a drip hitting the wood below.

"Well, that's a wrap." His old man crouched again and began placing all the junk he kept under the sink back in.

Shaw caught Atalee's horror at the way he stuffed it all haphazardly, with bottles of cleaning supplies tipping over and in no order whatsoever.

"Uh oh, Dad. You just sparked Atalee's organizational tendencies."

His father turned with a cocked brow and grinned when he saw her mouth open and her shaking her head.

"Seems you have a lot in common with my momma," she said.

"Oh, how is your momma?"

"Disorganized, possibly a hoarder."

They all laughed. Shaw's dad shoved in the last of the products and shut the cabinet door. "There, out of sight, out of mind."

"Oh God." Atalee groaned.

"Speaking of Atalee's mother, we thought we'd invite her over and grill some steaks if that's okay with you."

His father found his battered Stetson and plopped it on his head, nodding as he did. "Could go for a steak. There's some potato salad in the fridge."

"You made potato salad?" Shaw was dumbfounded.

He snorted. "You know me better'n that, boy. It's farm fresh. Bought it from the market down the road."

"So it's set. We'll go buy some steaks there later. Now, we thought we'd take the horses out to the creek. Exercise 'em."

His father bobbed his head. "They could use it. I got a mower to finish up before the guy picks it up for the weekend."

171

"We'll meet up in a few hours." Shaw sliced a look at Atalee. Damn, he was already burning for her and couldn't get her alone fast enough.

* * * * *

A fresh breeze washed over Atalee's bare skin, raising pleasing shivers in its wake. The perspiration from their lovemaking cooled all over her body, making her hyperaware of the man next to her.

She trailed her fingertips over the scar on Shaw's chest, down to the light fur leading to his groin. His stomach muscles twitched under her touch.

The man had thought of everything, even bringing along a clean quilt and a couple root beers in glass bottles which lay near the shore of the creek for the moment when they roused enough to drink them.

"Tell me about the guys you work with," she said out of the blue.

His chest rumbled. "What do you want to know?"

She thought on it. She only wanted to be brought into that part of his life—it was such a vital part of who Shaw was. "Well… are you friends with them?"

"Yeah. Some of us knew each other from the Texas Rangers. Now in many ways I feel like they're my brothers."

"That's fantastic. Do you see each other outside of missions?"

"We have a hangout. The Pins 'n Sins."

"The bowling joint?" She smiled against his shoulder, imagining these huge, bad-ass men slamming some balls and beers.

"Yeah, it's a good way to blow off steam."

"When can I come along?"

He tilted his head to see her where she lay sprawled across his chest.

"I mean..." She felt heat rise in her cheeks at her assumption. "Are girlfriends invited?"

"Nevaeh comes along all the time with Nash. You'll like her."

Atalee pushed upward to look at him. "Does that mean I can come next time?"

His blue eyes, his smile, the rugged angle of his jaw... all combined to thrill her as much as the warmth in his response. "I wouldn't leave you behind, baby doll. Now c'mere."

He hitched his arm around her. Before she understood his intention, he swept her up and leaped to his feet simultaneously. The world flashed by as he took three fast steps and then she was submerged in water.

Her head went under the surface and she didn't have time to sputter upward, because Shaw's hard lips crushed over hers. As she pressed closer into the kiss, he drew them both up and out of the depths. Her nose filled with air and the scent of her man.

Bringing her legs up around his waist, she rubbed against his erection. The length was slippery as he

173

brought the head to her needy entrance. Holding her breath, she anticipated the rush of sensation as he filled her. A gasp broke from her lips.

She clung to his neck as he dragged his cock in and out between her clenching walls. Ecstasy felt like a thousand flames licking at her insides. She angled her head and deepened the kiss, feeding him her tongue and gaining those delicious growls she knew so well now.

Ripples floated from around them in concentric circles. The sky overhead was so blue it almost hurt to look at.

And she was totally, utterly happy and in love.

Shaw yanked her up higher on his body, sinking deeper. Then he gently lowered her spine to the surface. "Can you float while I fuck you?"

"I can fly while you fuck me."

His grin flashed in his handsome face. She relaxed her torso to float on the surface as he grasped her hips and pulled her into him again and again until she felt too unsettled to remain still.

When he pulled her back into his arms and kissed her, she sank over his rigid cock, taking him to the hilt. He groaned, and she knew that sound coming from his lips by now — he was close to the edge.

Her pussy flooded. She squeezed her eyes shut and focused on the rhythm of Shaw moving inside of her.

He pressed his thumb over her clit, and she cried out. The throbbing amplified, singing through her veins. Her grip on his wet shoulders slipped, but he had her, anchored tightly to him, bound to him.

"Shaw!"

His low groan sent her shooting in an arc through the sky. Every pulsation that hit grew stronger until she lost herself completely in the man she loved. He pumped hot cum into her, letting loose and roaring his release in a way he never had before.

He went still, holding her as he emptied the last of his seed into her. When their gazes collided, they shared a grin. Then she giggled. "I've never heard you be so loud."

"Nobody can hear us out here. I guess all that holding back caught up to me."

"I liked it." She smiled wider. "We'll have to come out here more often."

His crooked grin cut a path through his rugged features, and somehow, her heart filled with even more love for him.

* * * * *

In front of him, Atalee navigated her horse down the narrow part of the trail, and Shaw watched her luscious ass rise and fall in the saddle. Damn, he couldn't get enough of her—had waited years for her. After believing she was lost to him forever, she was here with him.

Exploring her out in the open had been one of the highlights of his life, forever branded on his memory. Now they were headed back and then out to buy some rib-eyes for the grill.

Atalee drew her phone out and looked down at it, giving the horse his head for a moment.

"Everything all right?" Shaw asked.

"Just my mom verifying that she's just leaving home."

"I haven't seen your mother for a long time. Your brother either."

"We'll have to invite everyone 'round for dinner sometime." She pocketed her phone and took up the reins again.

Shaw watched the lines of her back, the artful way her hair waved over one shoulder. Damn, she really had no clue what she did to him, did she? That her offhand remark about having them around for dinner affected Shaw right to down to the tips of his boots.

They were doing this—together. She was making plans for them as a couple, even inviting herself along to nights at the Pins 'n Sins.

And he couldn't be happier.

She deserved a man who was home in her bed every night. A man who could be there to raise kids with her and love and support her each step of the way.

But fact was, in his line of work, he couldn't predict events.

Hell, he could go out tomorrow and never return.

Maybe she was right—he should return to the Texas Rangers, drop the special forces. It was still challenging and dangerous enough to give him a bit of the adrenaline rush he craved with better chances at staying alive long enough to grow old with the woman he loved and cherished.

But... letting down Sully, Linc and Lennon, Cav and Jess... hell, even Colonel Downs, was a difficult thought to touch on even for a second. Who would ever step into Shaw's shoes? The idea of Ranger Ops rolling on without him on their sixes...

Suddenly, she lifted a hand and waved. The path widened, and Shaw guided his horse beside her to see his father at the barn, watching them ride in. It hit him—what would his father say if Shaw asked his opinion on that life choice?

Once upon a time, he'd urged Shaw to take a leap—to let Atalee know his feelings. But in this matter, Shaw wasn't certain what his father's advice would be.

He reined up his horse and slid from the saddle. When Atalee followed, he was there to assist her, letting her slip through his hands to the ground. As they began to care for the horses, his father helped out to tuck them up with some hay, and they talked of the ranch and how it used to be.

His father looked over the field that used to be filled with livestock.

"Do you miss it, Dad?" Shaw rested a hand on his father's shoulder.

He was still a moment, then finally shook his head. "It was good for that time of life, but now I'm happy where I am. The work I have keeps me busy and better food on the table than my social security would provide. The horses I have left give me enough enjoyment." He smiled at Shaw.

Squeezing his father's shoulder, he moved to Atalee's side. "We're headin' down to the market for those steaks. Atalee's mother will be here soon."

"I'll make her welcome if she shows up before you're back. I've got that bottle of brandy."

"Thanks, Woody." Atalee leaned in and kissed Shaw's father on the cheek. When they walked away from him, he was still smiling.

"I think you made his day."

She laughed. "I know I made yours." After crawling out of the water, they'd drunk their root beers and she'd given him a show of sucking on the long-neck bottle — and then blown his mind by taking him in her mouth.

Shaw's bones still felt melted from that experience, and he planned to return the favor as soon as he had her all to himself again.

They got back into his classic car. The market was only a few miles up the road, a small business that remained alive out of necessity to the neighbors who didn't like to make longer trips into town.

"This place is so quaint."

"Got about ten aisles and two checkouts but the best cuts of steak around. C'mon."

They walked up to the front door, and he held it open for her. But the instant he did, the air hit him, charged with danger. If Shaw knew anything, it was that feeling.

Swiping his arm outward, he shoved Atalee behind him and scanned the scene before him.

Two guys wearing black bandannas over their faces old-Western robber-style had both cashiers at gunpoint.

As Shaw reached for the weapon he always carried concealed along his spine, he caught a small movement of one cashier as she pressed a fingertip into the screen of her phone.

Dialing 9-1-1.

His hackles raised. "Step back outside, Atalee. Slowly." When she didn't immediately move, he growled out, "Now."

Feeling her body heat move away from his back sent relief tingling through his veins. But he still had an issue to handle right in front of him.

"What's the trouble, guys?" He kept his voice nonchalant but the warm steel of his pistol grip felt good in his hand.

179

Both guys shot a look at him and then darted their gazes back to the cashiers. Judging from their appearance, they were young, twenties at best, and looking for some quick cash, even if there couldn't be much in those register drawers.

One's gun wavered, moving between the young woman behind the counter and Shaw as he sauntered over. "Stop walking! Stay still!" the guy barked out.

Shaw stopped.

"Let me see both your hands!" the kid called.

Shaw was aware of the crunch of tires on gravel outside the establishment. Either another customer was about to walk into this shit, or the state troopers had arrived. He hoped to hell Atalee was safely out of range.

"Guys, you don't want to do this. Believe me, prison is not as great as it seems on TV and once you're in the system, it's hard to be taken seriously even if you want to get out." Shaw kept talking as he moved up closer to the counter where he could protect the cashiers. The one closest to him was shaking so much that her sundress seemed to shiver in an invisible breeze.

"Put down the weapons and we'll end this, guys. You'll walk away with small-time sentencing and you'll still have a lifetime ahead of you to live." Shaw kept up his dialogue in slow, measured words, his gaze drinking in everything about these men right down to the set of their boots on the old wooden floorboards.

"Stop moving or I'll shoot you!" one guy yelled.

The door suddenly exploded inward and both men swung toward the commotion. Troopers stormed the space with weapons raised, barking orders. Shaw caught one's eye and noted that he recognized him. The trooper sliced a look behind Shaw where he held his weapon at the ready.

"Get back or we'll shoot these girls!" the other robber demanded.

Things happened too fast. The troopers surged forward. Shaw lunged at the women, knocking them both to the floor and out of firing range.

The troopers sent a volley of orders to drop the weapons and the boys refused.

And then he found himself standing between the troopers and the young kids, both arms flung outward.

"What the hell're ya doin', Woody?" The state trooper who'd recognized him pinched his brows together.

"Let's just calm things down here, okay? These young guys, they don't really want to lose their lives for a misstep like this. Do ya, boys?"

No response but he heard their labored breathing behind him. Before him, the troopers kept their weapons raised but with Shaw between them all, they weren't liable to shoot.

"Now everybody lower your weapons on the count of three and we'll discuss this like grown adults." He looked right, then left, at the faces of the young men, their eyes wide above the bandannas covering their faces. "Ready?"

One jerked his arm, and the state trooper yelled, "You try anything and I'll shoot you between the eyes! Set down your weapons!"

Shaw's gut clenched, and the sweat began to roll out from under his hat to drench the back of his neck. All at once, he was back in Mexico with a young person who'd made a bad life decision facing the loss of his life for his crime.

"Let's give them a chance to make the right decision." Shaw looked at them over his shoulders again. "All right, guys? On three. One, two…"

"Three," the trooper finished for him.

Two weapons rattled at Shaw's feet. In a lightning-swift move, he swiped them out of range, shoving them toward the troopers. Then he whirled on the guys, and he and the troopers converged on the criminals, taking them down to the floor in a blink and cuffing them.

Shaw's breathing came fast and rough. He'd done it—he'd fucking done what he'd failed to do back in Mexico and given these guys a choice. That kid Shaw had shot—he hadn't gotten one and Shaw would most likely remember that forever and hopefully continue to offer opportunities when possible.

That moment in Mexico, there hadn't been any choice. This time there was.

* * * * *

Atalee thrust her shaking hands under her arms and huddled around the side of the building. When she'd heard the shouting, her heart had stopped beating for what felt like a solid minute. Then it had restarted with a painful jerk in her chest.

Shaw. Please come back to me, Shaw. Please, God, don't let anything happen to him. I love him too much and I can't lose him.

Her pleas for his safety continued for long minutes after the troopers pulled up and stormed inside the market. And to think, they'd only come for steaks. If they'd been a minute sooner or later, they might have missed it all, but then again, Shaw wouldn't be in the thick of it.

Right where he wants to be, she realized. He was trained for events like this, and it was clear he was in his element.

His actions touched so many, kept so many safe in this world. Without him in the position he was in, how many would die? What atrocities would befall them?

She swallowed hard and brought one fist to her lips, fighting back the urge to scream his name and bring him running to her side. She knew if she called out for Shaw, he'd be with her in seconds and they could hurry away.

But that was the cowardly way, and he was no coward. So she had to be strong too, be worthy of him.

And she could not ever suggest he leave Ranger Ops, the job he loved, in order to find some alternative peace of mind, because fact was, the only peace of mind he could ever have was by fighting for what he believed in.

She loved a man who did dangerous work, and that was part of Shaw she couldn't ask him to abandon. She would take him as he was and love everything about him.

When the door banged open, she peeked out from her hiding spot to see the troopers bundling two men out of the market and Shaw right behind them. He glanced around for her, but she didn't step out. He'd only get angry with her for exposing herself to dangers before the men were securely locked in the backs of the squad cars.

She drew a hitching breath and let out an equally uneasy sigh. God, the things that might have happened to Shaw.

She looked at him again. He wasn't bleeding, at least. Something to be grateful for—she wouldn't be called upon to patch him up once they returned to his father's place.

The trooper closed the car door and turned to Shaw, hand out. Shaw gripped it hard and then the other man's as well.

They talked for a moment, but she couldn't make out their low, rumbling tones above the pounding of her heart. Shaw stepped away from them, and she emerged from her hiding spot. The moment their gazes locked, relief hit her like a tidal wave.

In a few steps, she was in his arms, and he held her shaking body tight to him, one hand cradling the back of her head. "Are you all right, baby doll?"

She nodded. "Are you?" She let her hands roam over him, feeling for blood she might have missed upon initial inspection.

"I'm fine. Oh shit. Hold on." He let her go and walked back inside. When he came back out with two big packs of steaks, she felt as if she'd cave in with relief.

Shaw caught her by the hand and led her to his car. On unsteady legs, she got in and waited for him to as well. He set the steaks behind his seat and looked at her. "Just a regular day in the life." He shrugged.

"I'm beginning to see that," she said in a whispery tone. She wet her lips. "Shaw, if you hadn't been there at the right time, who knows what could have happened!"

He rested a hand on her thigh, pinning her in the warmth of his touch. "I'm sorry, baby doll. That's the second time someone's had a weapon drawn around you, and I can't have you in danger."

"Neither time was your doing."

"It seems like trouble is drawn to me."

"Or you're drawn to trouble." She reached across the console and cupped his jaw, stubbled with beard. "Shaw, I was wrong to bring up the option of you leaving Ranger Ops. It needs you—you need it. I can't ask you to stop being you because I have selfish reasons. Whatever happens, I'll deal with it. I love you so much, and I can't ask you to change for me."

"I would, though." His eyes burned as he covered her hand with his strong one. "I love you enough to quit it all, Atalee."

She shook her head in awe. "I won't let you…"

He leaned in to brush his lips over hers, a quick meeting of mouths that spoke of promises to come. "I love you more for it, baby doll."

"We've been gone a long time," he said. "Our parents will think we stopped off for some roadside fun."

She half groaned, half giggled. "They'll think we're making up stories."

"At least we got the steaks. And…" He stopped, looking at her.

"What happened?" Her heartbeat picked up again when it had barely calmed enough.

"I think my reason for coming to you in the first place, Atalee… I'm pretty sure I'm past it now."

Searching his eyes, she understood. She took his face in her hands and brought him in for a kiss. "I'd like to take credit for helping you, but we both know it's not the case."

His lips, inches from hers, enticed. She stared at his mouth as he spoke. "You did help me. I owe you everything, and I plan to show you how much I appreciate you every day of your life. Starting with a big rare steak on the grill."

"Um... medium?"

"Damn, you know how to ruin a steak by overcooking." He flashed her a grin and started the engine, but her cylinders were already firing just from that smile he'd given her.

Chapter Ten

Atalee looked up from her computer screen at the rap on her door. Before she could get up to answer it or call out, her colleague came in. "Dr. Norman."

"Don't get up, Franklin. I'll have a sit down instead." He offered her a smile and sank to the seat opposite her desk. "I wanted to continue our discussion that was abruptly cut short the other day."

"Oh yes." She twisted away from her screen and gave her superior her undivided attention.

"How *is* your friend?"

"Um... He's actually a friend of a friend, but I hear he is being given top care."

He bobbed his head. "Good to hear. Troublesome, his injuries."

She dropped her gaze to her folded hands. "Yes, it is." Shaw had not told her much more about the entire mission and what exactly had happened to Linc, but he'd woken in the night and when she'd cuddled close to soothe him, his heart had been tripping hard and fast. The only thing he'd said when questioned was, "Linc. I got him out."

"Yes, you did," she'd responded, rubbing slow circles over his tense spine. Eventually he'd drifted off again, but it had taken her longer—it was easy to analyze ways to help him stop feeling responsible for every detail of everyone's lives.

Dr. Norman cleared his throat, and she gave him a pleasant smile. "What did you want to talk to me about?"

"As you know here in the city, we have an extensive homeless problem."

She nodded.

"And many of the homeless are veterans."

"Of course. It's a heartbreaking notion that the people who fought for our freedom can't find a place in our society."

He nodded, white hair gleaming under the office lighting and his expression grave. "I'm a vet myself, as you know. These are my brothers, and I want to help them."

"What can I do?" She leaned forward.

"I'm starting a group therapy, particularly for the homeless veterans, and I'd like you to assist me in running it."

Surprise washed over her, and she smiled in response.

"You like the thought," he commented.

She nodded. "I'm honored to work alongside you and learn even as we help these men and women. What are your thoughts on location?"

"Something centralized, accessible and comfortable enough that it isn't intimidating. We want these people to actually come in to talk about their problems and not feel judged or unworthy of stepping through the doors because they haven't showered and their clothes aren't clean."

An idea popped into her head. "Maybe we help with those things as well. Maybe by finding and partnering with a local YMCA or a gym that has showers *and* a room to meet in."

His eyes lit up. "Fantastic idea. I knew I wanted someone young with fresh ideas on this project. Now…"

For another half hour they brainstormed and exchanged ideas. The budget for the entire project was small, but she refused compensation for her time on this, feeling she was giving to the people who most deserved her time and all the hard work she'd put into her degree.

When they parted, Atalee felt hopeful about so much. Her professional life was following a path she was ecstatic about and she had the best thing going with Shaw, when she never believed she'd find a love like that.

Over steaks on the ranch, she and Shaw had talked and joked with her mom and his father, all of them enjoying the good food and wine. Bringing the people she and Shaw cared for together had made for such a fun afternoon, and she'd left feeling even closer to him.

Thinking of her momma reminded her that they still had some work to do on the room. Since Shaw would be wrapped up with Ranger Ops at a meeting, she was on her own.

She reached for her cell phone and dialed her mom. Slipping her hair over her shoulder, she brought the phone to her ear and waited for her mother to answer.

"Mom."

The line sounded with background noise.

"Hi, honey."

"Are you driving?"

"Yeah, I'm in the car. The traffic's heavy because they routed us around construction."

"I hear that. I was thinking I have time tonight to come over. Maybe we can finally finish your room."

"Oh, I'd like that, honey, but I'm on my way to someone else's house."

"Which friend?" Atalee shuffled paperwork to the side into a neater stack. Maybe she was finally finding some organization for herself—her desk no longer looked like an explosion had taken place in a paper factory.

A beat of silence followed, and Atalee said, "Mom?"

"I'm here. I'm going over to Woody's house, actually."

Atalee felt her eyes go round. "Shaw's dad?"

"I don't know of any other men named Woody, do you?"

She knew the Ranger Ops team called Shaw that, but no, she only knew one. Her mind tripped over their dinner the other night, backtracking for hints that something was happening between their parents that neither had caught on to, probably because they were both so in wrapped up in each other.

Her mother interrupted her thoughts. "I noticed when we were getting plates out that night that Woody's cupboards aren't very organized."

"Mom!" Shock hit. "Are you telling me that you're going over to his house to help organize his cupboards?"

"Well... He could certainly use some help. His bowls are sitting next to bags of potato chips and cookies, and there are about thirty plastic lids with no containers to put them on."

"What have I created?" Atalee shook her head in wonder.

"A monster, I guess. Anyway, I'll be home the other nights this week, so you and I can finish up my room."

"Mom."

"Yeah, honey?" She spoke over a horn blast from one of the cars in traffic.

"Could this have anything to do with Woody having nice blue eyes?"

"Oh Atalee! We aren't all easily persuaded by blue eyes. I'm just going to help, and Woody is easy to talk to as well. It's nice to have someone my age for company."

"Uh-huh." She wasn't buying it, now recalling how the two had exchanged a certain smile.

Wait. If their parents hooked up, would that make her and Shaw step-siblings? Oh God.

You're getting ahead of yourself.

"Have a safe drive. I'll talk to you soon, Momma."

"Love you, honey."

When they ended the call, Atalee drifted to her office window and looked down at the boring parking lot, her mind skimming over the many things she couldn't wait to tell Shaw.

Suddenly, she had an idea. Weeks ago, he'd taken a chance by showing up at her house and waiting for her to finish her run. It was time to turn the tables on her special ops man.

* * * * *

"Men." Colonel Downs strode into the room, and all five of the Ranger Ops jumped up to salute. Linc's empty seat around the shitty conference table left a hollow in the room, and each of them took turns darting looks at the chair, probably wondering as Shaw was how their buddy was faring in DC.

193

"At ease." Downs gave a hard nod to Sully. "How are things with Reed? Have you heard from him in DC?"

Sully widened his stance to give his report. "Heard from Linc yesterday, Colonel. He's receiving the best care. They've got his burns tended to and he's on the mend."

"Glad to hear it. Now, take your seats, gentlemen. I've got things to share."

Fuck, Shaw didn't like the sound of that. As he sank to the seat, he braced his elbows on the table and stared at their captain. Sully hadn't said a word about why they'd been called together today, but Shaw had his suspicions. For months, OFFSUS had been at odds with Homeland Security about whether or not Ranger Ops was essential. By now, he'd like to think they'd done a lot of fucking good in this part of the country and over the border. But it was hard to say if Homeland felt the same.

He caught Sully's eye, though his captain's face was blank and unreadable. Shit, he probably didn't know what was going on either.

This couldn't go well.

"Let me begin by stating you've all followed your orders to a T and gone above and beyond in the line of duty."

Fuck, here it comes.

Now that Shaw might be facing the dissolution of Ranger Ops, he realized he didn't want to return to regular duty as a Texas Ranger. After the adrenaline rushes, the victories—even the tough dips and valleys—he couldn't imagine not being with his team.

"I think you're all aware of what OFFSUS says about you."

"Could you refresh our memories, sir?" Lennon's voice held a note of strain that was most likely in part because his twin was in DC being patched back together.

The colonel shifted in his seat, looking down at the legs. "Damn, these chairs are real junk, aren't they? I'm going to stand to talk to you all." He did, and they all looked up to him.

"I've spoken with everybody but the President on this matter, it seems. And they've agreed to keep you together a while longer. We've got some shit brewing that could take Knight Ops away for a while, and that means we need you guarding the South."

"West," Cav drawled out.

Downs bit off a smile. "I'm not gettin' in on that old argument." There would always be someone with an opinion about whether Texas was in the West or South of the United States.

"Does this mean we can stop fearing that tomorrow we'll be unemployed, Colonel?" Sully asked point blank.

He gave a hesitant nod, which Shaw didn't feel confident about at all. "For now. This is a month by month, day by day thing, it seems. But know that I am fighting to keep you all here because I know the good you've done over the past months you were instated. With that said, I have two more things to say."

Shaw resisted the urge to tap his fingers on the table to hurry him along. The day by day thing with Ranger Ops and Homeland was pissing him off, but as there wasn't a thing they could do about it, he just wanted to head out, find Atalee and make the most of now.

"First, I'm going to see you guys have some better seating for meetings." Colonel Downs dipped his head to glare at the chair that had almost dumped his ass on the floor. He looked around at each of them. "And second, I'm sending ya'll a replacement until Reed is back on his feet."

Sully spoke up, "Who is it, sir?"

"Hawk from Team Rougarou." He flashed a grin. "Hope you're all ready for a bayou boy. Hawk's the best of the bunch, and you're sure to learn a thing or two from him."

"He's sure to find out we don't take shit from a swamp rat," Shaw drawled out, and they all laughed. Hawk was known all over the South and beyond for his tactical skills, and he was also part of the Knight family since he'd married their sister.

"He won't want to leave the Ranger Ops once he sees decent country and not swampland." Jess leaned back in his seat.

"All right, Ranger Ops. You'll meet up with Hawk in..." Colonel Downs glanced at his wristwatch, "two hours. You'll be receiving your orders before then."

Well, there went Shaw's plans to see his woman—in two hours he'd be shoved up the crack of some terrorist cell, trying to keep guns from getting in the hands of a bunch of nationalists with their eye on the governor again, recovering a truckload of humans who were being trafficked or God knew what else.

It was frustrating—but it was his job. And he fucking lived for it. Just as Atalee found passion in her profession, Shaw did too. She would understand all the missed holidays, anniversaries and nightly cuddles, wouldn't she?

Sully saw Downs to the door and then shot Shaw a look. "I'm running back to kiss my woman. You'd best do the same. Everyone, I'll see ya in a few."

"This Hawk guy better be able to handle his burritos," Jess remarked, getting up and heading for the door. "See you, assholes."

Shaw and the rest hurried out to get things in order before they rallied. The only thing he needed to take care of was locating his girl.

In the parking lot, he grabbed his cell and called her. She answered straightaway, her sweet voice filling his ear and sending love and desire through his body.

"Where are you?" she asked. "I came by your house. Are you still in your meeting?"

"Yeah, Downs was runnin' late. Look, baby doll, I'm being called out."

She fell silent. Damn, this was the hard part.

"I want to kiss you goodbye. Will you meet me?"

"Yes," she said at once. "Where?"

He named a place, a bit off grid in case he had a few spare minutes before heading back and getting geared up.

They hung up and the entire drive, his mind was flooded with thoughts of her. He was damn lucky to have her to kiss goodbye, and he needed to make sure she knew how much she meant to him.

When his phone rang, he grabbed it and glanced at the screen. "Atalee."

"Shaw, I can't make it." She was crying, her voice breathy with tears.

"What happened? What's wrong?"

"I'm stuck in this damn traffic routed around construction. I wasn't thinking or I would have taken another route—I only jumped in the car to head straight to you. Now, I don't know how long it will take. I'm going to miss you."

"Where are you?"

She named a part of town.

He cussed. That was difficult to pass through on a day of light traffic, let alone when it was congested as it was now.

"I'm sorry. I wanted to see you, but short of abandoning my car and running a few streets to catch a taxi..."

He chuckled, though ruefully. "It's all right, baby doll. I wanted to see you, you wanted to see me, but we'll make up for it the minute I'm back. Okay?"

She sniffled. "I love you, Shaw. Know that."

"I do. And I love you. When I come back, we're going to stay in bed for two days."

"Only two?"

He smiled. "As long as I can. Keep talkin' to me, baby doll. Tell me about your day."

While she spoke, he pulled over to the side of the road and listened to her voice oozing excitement as she told him about the homeless veteran group she and the head of the department were establishing. When she told Shaw about her idea to partner with a Y or a gym, he stopped her.

"There's a man you may have heard of. He was recently all over the news after he lost his job because he was slipping food out to the homeless. One of the other restaurants snagged him up, and you might be able to find him and see what he could do for you about providing some hot meals to your group."

"Oh my God, Shaw, you're brilliant! That is so helpful!"

"And I wanna help too. Actually, count us all in—the whole team. We'll fundraise for you or pitch in any way we can."

Her tears were back, and she gave a loud sniff. "You're amazing, all of you. You already give so much to the world and now this."

"It's a cause we can all stand behind. None of us want to be forgotten, and those guys might be at low points in life, but we can offer them hope and thanks and maybe a leg up."

"Shaw."

"Yeah, baby doll?"

"I love you."

"I love you too."

"Another thing."

"What's that?" he asked.

"When you come back, don't shave right away."

His cock stiffened immediately, thinking of rubbing his beard between her sensitive thighs while he licked her sweet juices from her pussy. "Deal. But you'd better meet me at the door in your birthday suit."

* * * * *

"Jesus Christ. Who did that?" Sully rolled down his window and Shaw's too with a tap of two fingertips. The SUV filled with noxious gas.

Shaw whipped around to see Lennon shaking with laughter and the other guys with hands over their faces to ward off the smell.

The other windows rolled down, and the Texas — God bless Texas — wind poured into the vehicle, though it took a while for the smell to leave.

"Hell, I need a lung transplant after that one. Man, your ass is foul," Hawk drawled. Cav reached over the seat to bump fists with him in agreement. After the fucking shit they'd just seen — and done — they had a new brother, an honorary member of Ranger Ops that would forever be one of them.

"You'd better shower after that one, Lennon." Shaw shot him a grin, feeling happy to be on the road home, with the Texas state line well behind them. He missed his stompin' ground, missed the big sky.

Missed the fuck outta his girl.

"Hell, I need a shower for just sittin' next to him. I can't go home to my wife smelling with that stench lingering on my clothes. Didn't your momma teach you better?" Hawk sent Lennon an accusing stare that only made the guy laugh.

"She did, but Linc and I reserve our manners for the ladies."

"At least you're not a guy who's rippin' one like that while in bed." Jess's comment had them all laughing again.

"When I get back, I'm heading straight for the pizza joint. I've been cravin' good stone-fired pizza since we left." Cav looked out his window.

"Man, you just ate a bag of Mexican food that would feed a family of six," Jess ribbed him.

"I could still eat. What are you doin' when you get back, Jess?" Cav asked.

"Hittin' the shower then hittin' my bed. Then hittin' some booty."

"Which one is it this time?" Lennon asked him.

"I don't have a special lady. They're *allll* special," he drawled out, sending laughter through the SUV again.

"Pins 'n Sins later this week?" Shaw threw them each a look. "Atalee asked to come along."

"Atalee doesn't know what she's getting herself into," Cav remarked from the very back.

Shaw grinned. "She doesn't. But I hope ya'll will go easy on her. Hawk, will you join us?"

"I'll be headin' back to Louisiana as soon as we debrief."

"Next time then."

"I'll take ya up on that." The man slanted a smile Shaw's way.

The rest of the drive was spent listening to more banter, but the closer they got to home, the more Atalee took up the majority of Shaw's thoughts. What had she been doing this past week? Had she gotten anything settled for her group of vets? Realizing he'd forgotten to fill in the guys on the fact that he'd volunteered them to help, he did now, explaining the cause.

Sully sent him a glance. "You know I'm in. Anything to help a brother."

Everyone agreed, and Shaw knew Atalee would be very happy to hear the news. He raised a hand to his stubbled jaw. She'd also be one exhausted woman after he spent hours between her sexy thighs...

Sully pulled the SUV into the parking lot of the building that served as their home base. When they walked inside, Shaw stopped dead in his tracks. His gaze fell over the new chairs circling the original table.

"Downs came through," he said.

"At least the man's fightin' our battles, one chair at a time," Jess commented, touching the back of one heavy wooden chair.

Then they each were called in to debrief and when Shaw was finally free, he found a new pep in his step, his energy restored at the thought of being with Atalee again.

He'd had a stressful week, and he couldn't wait to talk to his own sexy little therapist.

* * * * *

Atalee stood back to look around the room. From neat and tidy bookshelves to a new furniture unit with labeled baskets holding all of her mother's makeup so she could see exactly what she owned before buying more, the room soared above all the expectations Atalee had for it.

"Mom... we did it." The smile spread across her face. She touched the new lamp on a table they'd unearthed from the room that Atalee hadn't even known was here until they excavated it from beneath a pile of throw blankets. Next to the table was a cozy armchair they'd pushed and shoved into the space from her mother's bedroom that she never used.

"It's amazing. I never thought we could do it."

Atalee stared at her mother. "You worked all this time with me on a project you thought would fail?"

She chuckled. "I figured we'd both give up long before we completed it."

"Mom, that's shocking. I'm not a quitter!"

"You aren't. Look at how long you tried to keep things alive with Johnny."

Atalee stifled a groan at the mention of her ex. "I'm in such a better place now."

"You are. Oh honey, I'm happy for you, and happy that we had this time together. It was a weird sort of bonding experience, wasn't it?"

"More like a revelation that my mother is a hoarder."

Her mom balled up her fist and punched Atalee's upper arm. They both laughed and then hugged.

When they pulled away, they were a both a little misty-eyed. Atalee waved at the chair. "Well, test it out. Enjoy your new space. What are you calling it? An office? Den? Beauty room?"

"I think I'll call it my haven," she said, sinking to the armchair and crossing her legs as she looked around with satisfaction. "Now if I could get Woody to work with me on his kitchen as well as you and I work together, I'd be happy."

"Are you still going over to organize his cupboards?"

She nodded and splayed her fingers over her face, peeking out between them. "It's horrendous."

"Huh. I've seen something similar before." She widened her eyes at her mother, who only laughed and got up from the chair. She opened her mouth to say something else about how much time her mom had been spending over at the ranch with Shaw's dad, but her ring tone interrupted her.

She drew her phone out, thinking it could be work calling with an emergency, but her heart tumbled end over end as she saw who it was.

Her hand wavered as she hurried to bring the phone up. "Shaw!"

"Hello, baby doll. God, it's good to hear your voice."

His deep sugary drawl set her body on edge with only a few words. She half-turned away from her mother in order to hide the way her nipples pinched under her top.

"Where are you?"

"Headed to my place."

"Then I am too." She was already looking around for her purse but realized she'd left it at the front door. "Love you, Momma. I'll see you later." She leaned in to plant a kiss on her mother's amused face and practically ran to the front door.

"When you get here, I'll be in the shower. Waiting."

"I'm already wet." She lowered her voice as she hit the sidewalk, determined to get to her car and then to Shaw as fast as possible.

* * * * *

He opened the door in nothing but a towel.

Holy mother. I've hit the jackpot with this man.

Atalee's nipples bunched and her panties dampened as she looked him over from toe to head. Bare toes, lightly furred, strong legs cut off by the black towel that swathed his perfectly muscled hips. Above that, *the V* – the spot between abs and groin that made a woman fall to her knees. Broad chest dipping and swelling in all the right spots and shoulders a girl could latch on to and ride him long into the night.

She jerked her eyes upward. Short hair still wet from the shower, eyes dark with desire and a dark bruise looming up on his cheekbone.

She stopped there.

Stepping inside, she lifted her hand to skim her fingertips beneath the bruise. "God, I'm glad to see you."

He offered that casual smile, the slight tipping of the corner of his lips, but it was different too, softer. She'd seen his mouth in countless states—from tense, thinned lips to a sensuous parting as he lowered it to suck her nipple. Everything in between ran the gamut of hard and serious with the occasional quirk of a smile that quickly faded.

This one lingered as he stared down at her. Without a word, he encircled her in his arms and lifted her off her feet. She inhaled his fresh soapy scent and relaxed in his hold as he carried her to the bathroom. When he set her on her feet, he sank to his knees in front of her.

Her heart pounded as he stared up at her.

"I wanted to do this the day of your wedding. I fucking should have. Now I'm on both knees because you deserve more than just one."

Her throat closed off with emotion.

"I love you more than life, Atalee. It won't be easy for you if you choose to be my wife. I won't always be home, you'll sleep alone sometimes. I'll get hurt." He

207

gestured to his bruised cheek and then caught her hands in his.

When he brought them to his warm mouth, pressing a tender kiss to each, her insides knotted with want.

He looked into her eyes again. "But I promise to move mountains and rearrange oceans to make you happy, baby doll."

"Oh God, Shaw…" Her knees buckled and she landed before him with her arms looped around his neck. He tugged her up against his rock-hard body. Bringing her lips to his, she murmured, "Yes, I'll marry you."

From that moment on, her only goal was to return every kiss, touch and stroke of his mouth and hands. The shower forgotten, they ended up on the bathroom floor and his towel in a wad. As Atalee cupped his balls in one hand and guided his heavy erection to her lips, Shaw closed his eyes.

The first taste of his salty skin enticed her. A groan escaped her lips, and she sucked him fully in, savoring the grunt he made.

"Wait." His hand on her jaw had her looking up. His eyelids drooped over his blazing blue eyes. "Straddle my face."

Hot need ripped through her, and she never knew she could undress so quickly. When he planted his hands on her ass, spreading her apart and sinking his tongue deep into her pussy, she cried out in ecstasy. For a long minute as he sucked, licked and delved into her pussy, her mind blanked. Then she remembered where she'd left off.

Leaning over his muscled abs, she took his shaft into her mouth once more. The hard and soft feel of him between her lips drew her closer until his mushroomed head bumped the back of her throat.

Salty precum leaked onto her tongue. She swallowed around him, and he doubled his efforts on her pussy, tracing her outer lips up and down, drawing closer circles until he landed on her nubbin.

Her insides tightened and released rhythmically, each pulsation growing tighter, harder, more intense.

Breathing hard, she pulled on his cock with her lips and tongue. His hips bucked off the throw carpet they haphazardly had fallen over. Each groan she pulled from him with her mouth sent her higher and higher.

He dragged his finger through her wet folds, dipped into her entrance for a brief second and then moved upward... over her pucker.

Going still, she tried to wrap her mind around the brand new sensation.

He brushed over it with his fingertip again.

Drawing back on his cock, she ran her tongue around the edge. He tensed. "I'm close," he grated out.

"Good." She panted. "Because I'm about to explode. Do that again."

* * * * *

One more second of her sweet, hot mouth on him and Shaw wasn't going to last. He clamped his jaw for a harrowing second as he battled for control. Her flavors coated his tongue — all he wanted was more.

Grasping her hips, he hauled her down to his mouth again. Each flip of his tongue had her gasping around his shaft and his balls growing fuller. He had to tip her over the edge and fast so he could finish in her tight body.

He skimmed his finger over her ass, feeling a ripple run through her. Fuck, she was so untouched, so responsive to everything he did to her. Dipping his index finger into her wetness, he took a risk.

And sank it deep into her ass.

She came with a scream that resounded off the walls. With each contraction, he pumped his finger in and out of her ass while sucking her hard clit. Juices flooded over his mouth, and she shook against him, grinding her pussy down to get more.

When she increased the suction around his cock and took him into the back of her throat, his balls hitting her lips, white heat stole his sanity. The first jet of cum was huge, but she took it all, swallowing fast as he unloaded all the pent-up need he'd been harboring for days.

Slowly, he gave her one last lick and withdrew his finger from her ass. She collapsed atop him shamelessly, her head resting on his abs. It took him a long minute to regain his senses and find a way to breathe normally again.

"We didn't even make it to bed," she said.

"Yet." His dark tone offered only promises.

She shook with a small giggle. Love took over, and he found the strength to turn her into his arms, lift her and walk into the bedroom. They tumbled into the mattress, and he gathered her closer. With a coo, she tucked her head under his chin.

"I have a confession," she whispered.

He smoothed his hand over her spine to the dip of her waist. "What is it?"

"I've been wanting to suck your cock for days."

A growl left him, and he used a knuckle under her chin to bring her mouth to his. Tasting himself on her lips only made him harden all over again.

He barely got down to the business of kissing her when his phone gave a familiar chime.

Fuck, not right now. Not another mission.

He tore his mouth free. "I have to take this call."

She rolled away enough to free his arm and allow him to reach for the cell he'd left on his nightstand when he'd stripped and gone to the shower earlier. He brought it to his ear.

"Woodward."

"Hey, man." It was Sully—fuck.

"Tell me we aren't out again. We just fucking got back."

Sully chuckled. "Not yet. That I know of, anyway. I was calling to tell you to meet at Pins 'n Sins at seven."

"Shhiiiit, you asshole. You called to tell me to meet you for beer and bowling?"

Beside him, Atalee's face regained color and she flashed a smile. Looking at the glow of release still covering her beautiful curves, he wasn't sure he wanted to get out of bed today let alone face the public with the boner he was sure wouldn't go down anytime soon.

Their eyes met, and she nodded.

"We'll be there but we'll probably be late." He ended the call without waiting for his captain's reply, but knowing Sully, he'd be laughing right now.

Shaw drew her close again. "Where were we?"

"Here." She pressed her mouth into his, and he returned the soft pressure as the kiss tumbled from tenderness to passion and back again. She let out a sigh and snuggled close.

After a heartbeat of silence, she said, "I have something else to tell you."

"You're full of surprises today, aren't you?" He wasn't worried—anything she told him, they'd handle together.

"Have you talked to your father lately?" she asked.

His heart gave a short jerk as if someone had it by a rope and given it a tug. "No. Is everything okay?"

"Yes. I'm sorry if I just worried you. But yes, he's fine. At least my mother says so…"

"Wait. Your mother?" Everything came together in his mind. "Are they spending time together?"

"She claims she's helping him organize his house, but I have a feeling something else is brewing."

Shaw arched a brow.

She smacked at his shoulder. "Don't even suggest it, Shaw! I can't think of my mother doing that!"

Chuckling, he rolled her onto her back and buried his face between her breasts, nuzzling from one to the other until her nipples were sharp peaks of desire again. "I hope you can think of me doing this to you for the rest of our lives."

She ran her thumb over his bearded jaw. "This and so much more." Her eyes twinkled. "That thing you did to me in the bathroom?"

God, was she really going to say she wanted him to take her in the ass?

He nodded.

She leaned in and whispered in his ear. His cock lengthened to hard steel, and with a groan of need, he flipped her onto her stomach with her perky ass hiked up in the air.

Epilogue

The big ranch house was decked inside and out with flowers and gold wedding décor. The low notes of a classical guitar drifted through the open window, coming from the garden behind the house.

Atalee beamed at her friend Nevaeh. "You're stunning. Nash is going to fall over dead when you walk down that aisle."

Nevaeh directed a dark curl over her shoulder. "Okay, I'm ready to see myself. Turn me around." Her ballgown with a mini train was full-on Texas bride, but she'd been far from a Bridezilla during all the preparations and been nothing but sweet to all who helped her.

Together with Nevaeh's mother, Atalee helped to guide the train around into position as her mother spun her to face the full-length standing mirror.

As soon as Nevaeh saw her reflection, she teared up.

"Oh Lawdy, somebody fan her!" Atalee ran to the dresser and grabbed a binder that held the menus the bride and groom had chosen from and began waving it in front of her friend's face.

"You're right, Atalee—Nash is going to fall over! I can't believe this is me." She stared at the mirror again. "Actually, I can't believe this is my life at all." She looked around at the master bedroom that was newly remodeled to accommodate the owners. She and Nash had inherited the home from Nash's dear old friend who'd recently died serving as a Texas Ranger.

"Good things come to good people." Atalee grinned at her friend.

"Okay, you can stop fanning. I'm all right for now—until I see Nash. Oh Atalee, wait till you walk down that aisle to Shaw."

The four of them had become pretty close over the past few months, and Nevaeh knew everything about her first marriage and her worries about tying the knot again. But deep down, she knew this time it was right. Nothing could stop her when they finally decided to set the date.

She handed Nevaeh her bouquet of spray roses and tiny gold pearls. "Now you're ready. I hear the song ending."

Nevaeh made it out of the room in a flurry of bling and skirts with Atalee behind her positioning her train. A shadow fell over her, and she looked up to see the most handsome man in a gorgeous tuxedo she'd ever seen.

Slowly, she straightened on her high heels and leaned in to sniff Shaw's cologne. "God, you smell delicious."

His crooked smile had her stomach doing somersaults. "You're beautiful." He took her hand and brought her ring finger to his lips. The heat of his mouth sank deep into her, and she pressed her thighs together.

"Don't get me too worked up, Shaw. I have to walk out in a minute. Actually, what are you doing here? You're supposed to be up there with N—!"

Her sentence was cut off as he yanked her in and crushed his mouth over hers. The music, his scent and the moment swelled inside her.

When she pulled away, they stared into each other's eyes. "Let's set that date later, okay?"

"'Bout time. I've been waitin' on you, baby doll." He squeezed her hand and disappeared. A minute later, he was standing up beside the groom. The music changed again, and Atalee prepared to walk the white silk aisle of fabric that cut through the lavish garden.

She looked up and found her lover's intense gaze on her. She smiled and started up the aisle. Soon it would be to the right—the perfect—man.

THE END

Em Petrova was raised by hippies in the wilds of Pennsylvania but told her parents at the age of four she wanted to be a gypsy when she grew up. She has a soft spot for babies, puppies and 90s Grunge music and believes in Bigfoot and aliens. She started writing at the age of twelve and prides herself on making her characters larger than life and her sex scenes hotter than hot.

She burst into the world of publishing in 2010 after having five beautiful bambinos and figuring they were old enough to get their own snacks while she pounds away at the keys. In her not-so-spare time, she is fur-mommy to a Labradoodle named Daisy Hasselhoff.

Find Em Petrova at empetrova.com

Other Titles by Em Petrova

Ranger Ops
AT CLOSE RANGE
WITHIN RANGE
POINT BLANK RANGE

Knight Ops Series
ALL KNIGHTER
HEAT OF THE KNIGHT
HOT LOUISIANA KNIGHT

AFTER MIDKNIGHT

KNIGHT SHIFT

ANGEL OF THE KNIGHT

O CHRISTMAS KNIGHT

Wild West Series

SOMETHING ABOUT A LAWMAN

SOMETHING ABOUT A SHERIFF

SOMETHING ABOUT A BOUNTY HUNTER

SOMETHING ABOUT A MOUNTAIN MAN

Operation Cowboy Series

KICKIN' UP DUST

SPURS AND SURRENDER

The Boot Knockers Ranch Series

PUSHIN' BUTTONS

BODY LANGUAGE

REINING MEN

ROPIN' HEARTS

ROPE BURN

COWBOY NOT INCLUDED

The Boot Knockers Ranch Montana

COWBOY BY CANDLELIGHT

THE BOOT KNOCKER'S BABY

ROPIN' A ROMEO

Country Fever Series
HARD RIDIN'
LIP LOCK
UNBROKEN
SOMETHIN' DIRTY

Rope 'n Ride Series
BUCK
RYDER
RIDGE
WEST
LANE
WYNONNA

Rope 'n Ride On Series
JINGLE BOOTS
DOUBLE DIPPIN
LICKS AND PROMISES
A COWBOY FOR CHRISTMAS
LIPSTICK 'N LEAD

The Dalton Boys
COWBOY CRAZY Hank's story

COWBOY BARGAIN Cash's story
COWBOY CRUSHIN' Witt's story
COWBOY SECRET Beck's story
COWBOY RUSH Kade's Story
COWBOY MISTLETOE a Christmas novella
COWBOY FLIRTATION Ford's story
COWBOY TEMPTATION Easton's story
COWBOY SURPRISE Justus's story

Single Titles and Boxes
STRANDED AND STRADDLED
LASSO MY HEART
SINFUL HEARTS
FALLEN

Club Ties Series
LOVE TIES
HEART TIES
MARKED AS HIS
SOUL TIES
ACE'S WILD

Firehouse 5 Series
ONE FIERY NIGHT
CONTROLLED BURN
SMOLDERING HEARTS

The Quick and the Hot Series
DALLAS NIGHTS
SLICK RIDER
SPURRED ON

EM PETROVA
WWW.EMPETROVA.COM